OF WOLVES AND MEN

G.A.HAUSER

Of Wolves and Men

G. A. Hauser

Of Wolves and Men

OF WOLVES AND MEN

Copyright © G.A. Hauser, 2011

Cover design by Colt St. John

Cover model; Jimmy Thomas

www.romancenovelcovers.com

Edited by Stacey Rhodes

Artwork; G. A. Hauser

Special Thanks to LM St Claire

ISBN Trade paperback: 978-1461-0201-4-1

The G.A. Hauser Collection LLC

This is a work of fiction and any resemblance to persons, living or dead, or business establishments, events or locales is coincidental.

All Rights Are Reserved. No part of this may be used or reproduced in any manner whatsoever without written permission, except in the case of brief quotations embodied in critical articles and reviews.

WARNING

G. A. Hauser

This book contains material that maybe offensive to some: graphic language, homosexual relations, adult situations. Please store your books carefully where they cannot be accessed by underage readers.

First The G.A. Hauser Collection LLC publication:
April 2011

Have mercy on the wolf for he is one with his heart and spirit just like his human brothers.

G. A. Hauser

Chapter 1

Charlie Mosby pulled his pickup truck into the long, dusty gravel driveway of the ranch where he worked. Sixty horses, three managers, and ten wranglers were under his supervision.

Even in early November, dry dust stirred up behind his tires as he stopped, hopping out. During the day the temperatures weren't that bad. Lately they were between forty and fifty. At night it was beginning to hit freezing. Some nights near the teens.

His truck bed and trailer were loaded up with hay and oats. "Butch! JP! Goat! Git yer asses over here." Charlie took off his cowboy hat and whacked it against his jeans, sending up more dusty plumes. He had on a heavily-lined sheepskin leather jacket, which kept him warm all winter, along with his snakeskin boots.

Butch Crowell and JP Martin jogged over to help unload the trailer, with the third of their number struggling to keep up.

"Come on, Goat. Give it some effort." Charlie gave Hal 'Goat' Groates and shake of the head.

Without having to say another word, the three men began transferring the bales of hay and bags of oats to the stable. The daytime wranglers had arrived and were cleaning out the barn.

Charlie left them to their work and walked up the two wooden steps to the ranch home. It had a grand front porch which was the entire length of the house and wrapped around south side. In the summer it was loaded with rocking chairs, benches, and outdoor dining tables. The home was the heart of the forty acre ranch and where the owners Vernon and Connie Norman lived. The property line butted up against the Deer Creek reservoir and federal parkland. The view of the Wasatch Mountains beyond was spectacular, even from the one bedroom cabin Charlie resided in.

"Vernon?" Charlie glanced around the room with the high vaulted ceiling and a fireplace, lit and roaring, warming the room. The hearth took over the entire wall with its exposed rock chimney reaching to the roof.

"Yeah, Charlie?"

"Got the boys unloading the hay." Charlie walked closer to his boss after spotting him eating lunch with his wife, Connie. "Howdy, ma'am."

"Hello, Charlie. You want something to eat?"

"Up to you. I can eat with the boys." Charlie used his hat to gesture to the front door.

"Sit." She removed a plate from the cupboard.

Charlie put his hat down, tossed his coat over a chair in the living room, and washed his hands at the sink. "I'm grateful, ma'am. I'm very hungry."

"You tell the boys when they're done to come get some lunch."

"I will do." Charlie sat beside Vernon who was using his fingers to help push a wedge of steak and mashed potatoes onto his fork.

Charlie heard his stomach grumble. *Nothing but the best food to eat at this ranch.* The money Vernon and Connie made during the year renting out cabins and having horse riding ventures made them wealthy people.

Charlie had no complaints. He was treated like a son, had room and board included with his pay, and loved the work.

"Here you go, Charlie."

"Thank you, ma'am. Looks great." He picked up the serrated knife and it sunk into the meat like through butter.

Once Connie joined them, making sure everything was on the table, Vernon said to Charlie, "Something's out at the west end of the property ripping up the fence line."

Charlie swallowed his steak with a gulp of bottled beer and sat up. "When's this started?"

"Far as I know, last night. One of the wranglers was doing a perimeter ride and came up on a hole in the barbed wire."

"Me and Butch will head up there after lunch."

"Thanks, Charlie. Probably some pranksters, but if it's a cougar or bear, we need to know."

Nodding, Charlie said, "I got it covered, boss."

Though the three engaged in light conversation, Charlie was preoccupied. He didn't like anything upsetting the balance of this ranch. The sixty horses were all in good health, they had a great snowshoeing and trail riding winter season to look forward to, and last summer the rodeo at Deseret Peak gave them a ton of referral business.

He politely waited until both Connie and Vernon were done eating before carrying his plate to the sink. "Thank ya, ma'am." Charlie put his hat and coat on. "Always a treat to be invited to your table."

"Anytime, Charlie. We don't know what we would do without you." Connie smiled sweetly. "You're like the son we never had."

Charlie thought about their two daughters, Suzie and Sherlane, both in college, one in Boston, the other in Palo Alto. The girls were expected home for winter break, but neither had shown up yet. At twenty-five Charlie did have some idea of finding a nice woman to settle down with...at least he had until the incident last October.

His truck had got a flat tire along Interstate 80 and a man had stopped to help him fix it. *Joe.*

Charlie shook himself out of the memory, wondering if it had opened a door to the other side of the 'sexual norm' that had never been meant to be opened.

He stepped outside after putting on his hat and coat. Charlie's truck bed and trailer were empty of bales of hay. Butch was sweeping it out while JP and Goat were still inside the barn.

"Hey, Butch."

"Yeah, Charlie?"

"After you boys get a bite, you and me have to ride to the west fence line."

"I heard the wire was cut."

"That's right. Go eat. I'll saddle up the horses."

Butch hopped down from the truck, walking into the barn with Charlie. "So many jerks camping out there. I bet they just fucked it up to be smart." Butch hung the broom up by the hole in the handle along with other tools neatly arranged.

"JP, Goat, go get some grub." Charlie thumbed over his shoulder.

"Good. I'm starving." Goat brushed off his hands on his jeans.

"Yer always starved." JP whacked his arm.

"He got enough meat on his bones to keep him alive for a week." Butch laughed. He said to Charlie, "Be a minute."

"I'll be here." Charlie stared at Butch's ass as he walked, turning away before anyone noticed. Out of the three men who were permanent employees, Butch was the cutest...and youngest. All of nineteen. JP was thirty-eight, divorced twice with kids from each marriage, and Goat was a big ole bear, shy to everyone's gaze. Charlie wouldn't be surprised if he was a virgin.

But no gay boys here. None.

What did you do to me, Joe? Charlie walked to a stall and removed his horse. "Heya, big boy." He rubbed Spirit's white blaze, removing the tall, sixteen hand chestnut gelding from the stall. The horse snorted and nodded his head.

"You and me are goin' for a ride." He led the big animal to the ring on a wall, taking off the halter and easily fitting a bridle. Spirit and Charlie were like brothers. Neither gave the other one any grief, just love. As Spirit chewed on the bit, getting it comfy in his mouth, Charlie brushed him just because he wanted to. Butch would take a while to eat anyway.

"How's my big fella?" As Charlie ran a curry comb over Spirit's thickening winter, rusty-brown coat, he had an image of Joe's head bobbing on his lap in his truck. Charlie stopped what he was doing to recall that act. After Joe had helped him change the flat tire, Joe had actually asked if he could suck Charlie's cock. He'd known Joe had to be gay. He had an earring in his ear, spiky dyed blond hair, a slight effeminate quality to him that Charlie recognized immediately as homosexual, and Joe was obvious in expressing his attraction to his cowboy looks. *Not to mention, Joe was very pretty.*

Charlie blushed at the thought. *Best blowjob I ever did get.*

Spirit looked back at him, as if asking, *You going to keep brushing me or what?*

Charlie continued where he'd left off. *Yeah, but, am I gay now? One handsome man sucks my cock in my truck and... Presto? Gay? Now I want a man? What do I want?*

He thought he knew. He also never expected to have to reenact that event every night so he could come before he slept. It was bad enough hearing the teasing about *Brokeback Mountain* from the tourists. It never failed. When they saw him and Butch standing together they mentioned that movie. The East and West Coast city women would go all gaga and take pictures of the two of them with their horses.

Of Wolves and Men

Charlie didn't think he was ugly, but he didn't think he was a movie star either.

He tossed the curry comb into a box of grooming tools, taking a saddle off the hook.

A scuff of a boot made him turn to look. "You didn't have to eat that fast, Butch."

"I always do. And that spot in the fence is bugging me." He took his horse out of its stall—Scout, a sturdy pinto, mostly white with brown spots and a brown mane and tail.

While Charlie tightened the cinch, he couldn't help but peek at Butch as he got Scout ready. But he wouldn't be caught dead looking at Butch in a seductive way. Butch wasn't gay. Charlie knew that much. But then again, he'd never considered himself gay or bi-curious until Joe's amazing mouth and tongue made him come like he had never come in his life.

After he loaded up tools, a shotgun, and wire fencing, Charlie hoisted himself into the saddle and waited. The temperatures were making all of them blow out steam clouds with their exhaled breaths.

A moment later, Butch was behind him in his own saddle, nodding his head in a gesture to go. Harley, the hyperactive Jack Russell terrier, barked under the horses' legs. The geldings were used to him and didn't flinch.

"Get back in the house, Harley," Butch hollered, but the dog did what he wanted to do regardless.

Charlie didn't care if the dog wanted to tag along. Harley may be small, but he wouldn't hesitate to challenge a black bear and chase it off.

Deep in his thoughts, Charlie listened to Scout's clip-clop in time with Spirit's. There was no rush. The hole in the fence wasn't going anywhere and the ranch's horses were all in enclosed paddocks while their stalls were being cleaned.

November evenings the temperatures varied. October had been so mild, no one knew when the deep freeze would finally hit. So far the cold was tolerable. They could ride until dusk without the painful wind-chill making their skin red.

"All I got from Vernon was west side." Charlie slowed Spirit down to allow Scout to catch up. Harley was sniffing and running ahead of them on the trail.

"I have an idea where."

Charlie stared at Butch's profile in his cowboy hat for a moment, turning away before Butch noticed his gaze.

After twenty minutes of riding at an easy pace, Butch pointed ahead of them. "I think it's right beyond those trees."

Harley began barking and raced to the direction Butch had indicated. It put both men on the alert. "What's he got? Bear?"

"Don't know." Butch pulled his shotgun out of its holster on the saddle and held it as they approached.

As he drew closer, Charlie could see the hole in the fence. It was a huge gap he wasn't prepared for. "I thought it was gonna be a small tear. What the fuck?"

"Harley!" Getting off of Scout, Butch cocked the shotgun, jogging to where the dog was going crazy.

Charlie did the same, taking his own gun as they chased the frantic dog. When they got to where Harley was making a ruckus, they found nothing but a deer carcass.

Charlie took a closer look at it. "Cougar kill this?"

Butch knelt down. "I never seen a cougar do that. That ain't right."

Standing, Charlie scanned the area. A few birds circled—carrion eaters, obviously catching a scent of death. "I swear if I find some devil worshipping thing going on here," Charlie said, fuming, "I will shoot first and ask questions later."

"Naw. Up here? Them morons won't come up here. They'll freeze their asses off here at night." Butch unloaded the twelve gauge shell then slid the shotgun back into its place on the saddle. He removed the barbed wire they had brought and the tools to get the hole repaired.

"First they kill a deer, then it'll be our ponies." Charlie set his gun nearby, in case. Harley kept sniffing the area around the dead doe, but seemed to have calmed down.

"I still think an animal could have done that. We got so many coyotes now. Could be anything. Christ, Charlie, could be a pack of feral dogs."

"Can't be wolves. Ain't no wolves up here no more. It's got to be a bear or cougar or somethin'."

Quietly they worked on patching the fence, Charlie was still slightly uneasy. The deer didn't look like it was killed by a natural predator. He'd seen enough to know. What it looked like to him was it had been sliced up with a knife, and afterwards, animals had begun to feed on it.

His hands began to get cold as the sun lowered down the western skyline. He glanced back at the horses. They were chewing the long dried grass, appearing content.

A crow or large black bird landed near them on a fence post. Charlie would never have expected it to alight so close to where they worked. He said to the bird, "You'll have your meal back. Give us a minute."

The bird cocked its head sideways, meeting Charlie's eye like he had never had a bird do before.

"Shoo!" Charlie waved his hand. *That damned thing is making me nervous.*

Butch turned to look, laughing. "You can't even scare a crow. Pathetic."

"That ain't no crow." Charlie's gestures did nothing to intimidate the large black bird.

"Ignore it." Butch made a hissing noise and flinched in pain, sucking his finger. "Fucking barbed wire."

"Where're your gloves at, you dipshit?" Charlie glanced at the bird. He figured Butch's abrupt reaction would scare it off. If anything, it had moved closer. He checked on Harley. "Hey, Harley. Go bark at that nosy bird."

The dog ignored him, lifting his leg on a nearby tree.

Butch kept his finger in his mouth as he said, "Will you forget the darn crow?"

Charlie continued to use pliers to repair the fence, keeping his eye on the pitch black iris of the watching bird.

Butch stood, taking his gloves out of his jacket pocket and putting them on.

Charlie watched to see if his actions would startle the crow. "That is seriously weird." Charlie straightened his back and began approaching it.

"What are ya doing?" Butch asked.

Ignoring him, Charlie closed the gap between him and the bizarre bird. They were a mere two feet apart. "Why aren't you flying off?"

The bird cocked its head sideways again, ruffling its neck feathers.

"You dumb thing. I can catch you and put you in a cage."

A loud squawk coming from the bird made Charlie jump. He heard Butch's laugher behind him.

Charlie whispered so Butch couldn't hear, "You laughing at me? You think I'm too scared to catch you?"

The bird inched closer, jumping off the post to the wire, its black feet and long, black talons clasping it as it moved.

Charlie was so stunned, he stood still seeing how close the bird would come. When it was nearly beside him, the bird extended an impressive wingspan, scaring Charlie to death. "Boo?" he said, nervous as hell.

Again the bird let out a cackle that sounded so much like laughter, Charlie got chills up his spine.

"Mosby, if you don't get over here and help me with this fence, I'll tell all the boys ya got scared of a crow."

Of Wolves and Men

Charlie backed up, keeping his eye on the bird. He pointed at it. "Don't be doing nothin' behind my back, ya hear?" He returned to finish fixing the fence. "That bird is smiling at me. It's freakin' me the fuck out."

"You're an idiot." Butch laughed, wrapping the wires around nails.

Harley finally decided to give the men his attention. Butch gave him a rub down on his ears, then pointed to the bird. "Harley, go chase that thing off, it's scaring baby Charlie."

Before Charlie could reply, Butch gave Harley a nudge towards the ominous bird.

Harley got one look at it and yelped, hightailing his way back to the ranch.

Butch and Charlie exchanged surprised glances. "That dog doesn't run from nothin'!" Butch said.

"Let's just get this done." Charlie tried to ignore the crow but it wasn't easy.

After an hour of repair work, Charlie loaded up his tools and removed more items from the saddle.

"You are not taking that thing with us."

Charlie ignored Butch's protests, using a plastic tarp to secure the carcass to a rope. "I am."

"I thought you were the sane one out of us, Charlie. I don't know what's come over you." Butch loaded up the tools, strapping the saddle pouch's buckles tight.

Tying the rope to the back of Spirit's saddle, Charlie gave it a tug. Spirit looked uneasy with the new load, shifting and snorting twin blasts of steam into the cooling air.

They were losing daylight and needed to head back.

Charlie put his foot in the stirrup and swung his leg up and over the horse, picking up the reins. He looked back at the blue-wrapped deer carcass they were dragging, and then did a last scan for the crow. It was gone. Charlie didn't know when it had left, but was glad it had.

He tapped Spirit with his boot heels and made a noise to let him know to begin their trek back. Butch was quiet as he followed behind, as if keeping tabs on the dead deer.

Charlie began to daydream as he rode; the season of snow and ice ahead, working hard to make sure the animals were well fed cared for in the upcoming months…

The horse snorted, waking him from his stupor. He gave the twilight sky a scan. It was beautiful, with pinkish purple wisps of clouds behind the hilly landscape. Just as he was about to get lost in his thoughts once more, he caught sight of a dark shape moving between pine trees. It could have been anything; elk, pronghorn, cougar, bison, moose… The wildlife in this area was plentiful. It's what Charlie loved most about living in the area.

A set of glowing green eyes nearly scared him do death.

Charlie asked Butch, "What's that over there?"

"Where?"

"There!" Charlie lost sight of it.

"More crows?" Butch laughed.

"Never mind." The rest of the way Charlie felt as if he was being watched, followed, but he knew he was just being stupid.

Chapter 2

By the time he and Butch arrived back at the barn it was nearing five. He made sure Spirit was well tended before his attention was involved with more urgent matters. In the next stall, Butch was doing the same to Scout, settling him in for the night. Charlie could hear Butch's low murmuring, talking to the sturdy painted horse. He smiled. Everyone who worked this ranch had a soft spot for horses, and each man had his own to baby.

Charlie gave Spirit a sugar cube and a last pat on the head. He backed out and closed the door and bolt.

"What the hell are ya going to do with that?" Butch pointed to the wrapped carcass.

"I'm going to call Doc McMurray." He took his mobile phone out and checked his watch.

"She'll be eating dinner."

"Shut up and go away." Charlie put the phone to his ear.

Butch stayed quiet but stood by.

"Doc, it's Charlie over at the Norman Ranch."

"Hello, Charlie, what can I do for you?"

"I hope I didn't catch ya at a bad time."

"You don't worry. Are the horses all right?"

"Yeah, knock wood." Charlie rapped his knuckles on a thick support stud. "I found me a deer up in the woods when I was fixing the fencing."

"She hurt?"

"No, Doc, she's dead. But the way she died…that's what worries me." He peeked at Butch who was gazing at the blue tarp.

"What do you mean, Charlie?"

"I have a bad feeling, you know? Like some stupid satanic cult is at something. Can you take a look at her?"

"I will. That kind of thing troubles me as much as you. Can you bring her here, or do you want me to come there and you can show me where it is?"

"I drug her down the mountain here to the barn. I'll load her up in the truck."

"I'll be expecting you."

"Thanks, Doc." Charlie put the phone into his pocket.

"I'll help you out."

"Go tell Vernon first."

Butch jogged out of the barn. Charlie sighed, feeling heavy in his heart. They didn't need this. He took his keys out of his pocket and unhooked the trailer from his pickup, before backing it up to the barn to make it easier to load the dead doe.

Vernon, Connie, and the boys appeared, rushed and worried.

"Let me see her first." Vernon pointed to the blue tarp.

Goat and JP knelt down to untie the lacings while Connie wrapped her wool coat tightly around her, looking very upset.

JP opened the tarp with Goat's help and each made a noise of disgust when they saw the deer.

Vernon inspected it. "I don't like this one bit."

"Right by the hole in the fence, boss," Butch said, scratching his head under his hat.

"Vernon," Connie said, her voice quaking, "We have to tell the sheriff about this."

JP wrapped the tarp up and tied it.

"I'm taking it to Dr. McMurray's place. Let's see what she says." Charlie gestured to the three other men to help him lift the carcass to the bed of his truck. He counted, "One, two, three," and they heaved it up together.

Butch shut the tailgate with a clang.

"So that's it?" Vernon asked, Charlie, "Just the hole in the fence and this deer?"

"Ain't no hole, boss," Charlie shook his head as he said, "Was a huge gap. When you first mentioned it, I thought we had a tear. It was no small tear."

Butch added, "Five, six feet of open barbed wire."

"Son of a bitch!" Goat said.

"Right." Vernon nodded. "I'll call the sheriff's office and you let me know what Hope has to say."

"I will, boss." Charlie hopped into the truck.

Butch got in beside him.

"You don't have to come. Go eat dinner."

"How're you going to get that out alone?" He gestured to the deer in the truck bed.

"Draggin' it out is the easy part."

"Go." Butch buckled his seatbelt.

They drove, country music playing on the radio. Neither was in a singing mood however. Charlie kept losing track of his thoughts. Worrying about the trouble they may be in if some strange cult decided to hit their ranch wasn't going to help any of them. They would alert the authorities and beef up their own patrols at night. He would be the first to volunteer to head up the mountain and keep an eye out.

Butch shifted on the seat, leaning his elbow on the armrest.

Charlie stole a glance at his crotch. *Joe sucked my cock right here. Right here where I'm sittin'.*

He and Joe had both been dirty from lying under the truck on the side of the highway. The tire had fallen on Joe when it released from under the rig. Charlie recalled his hairless chest when he raised up his shirt to see the damage. But it was the blowjob he couldn't stop thinking about. *That fucking hot sucking, his tongue going wild, the moaning as if the guy really liked it, even though I was sweaty and all...*

"Here. Turn here!" Butch pointed. "Christ, Charlie, where are you in that head of yours?"

Charlie wouldn't answer that question even with a branding iron aimed at his behind.

He stopped the truck and immediately Dr. Hope McMurray and her husband Ralph exited the house, as if they'd been waiting for them.

Charlie shut off the engine and got out quickly, meeting them and opening the tailgate. "Where should we bring it?"

"In there." Hope pointed to an outbuilding she used for quarantined animals. Charlie knew it well from when one of the horses had an unknown infection last summer.

With Ralph's help, he and Butch dragged the blue tarp to the lit up area inside the building. Immediately she put on rubber gloves and a mask.

Charlie and Butch unlaced the tarp and opened it up, stepping back.

"Holy crap." Ralph recoiled. "That isn't from a cougar or bear."

"No." Hope inspected the tissue. "It's from a knife."

As she dug into the entrails, Butch covered his mouth in reflex. Charlie wasn't as queasy since he'd seen the horses with ugly injuries before. Butch hadn't been on the ranch long enough to see what they could do to themselves when spooked or attacked.

"Heart's missing. Classic sign of a ritual killing." Hope appeared grim.

"No!" Butch stomped his foot. "Hell no! Not around here, not on our ranch!"

"Calm down, buddy." Charlie felt the same way but someone head to keep their head.

She continued to poke and inspect the entrails. "The lungs are missing as well, but they don't look cut out. Maybe a scavenger has eaten them. It's not unusual for the internal organs of a dead animal to be eaten first."

Charlie noticed Butch about to explode. He moved closer to him. "We'll figure it out. Okay?"

"Yeah." He spoke softly but he looked furious.

Ralph asked, "Did you already report it to the sheriff's office?"

"Vernon is. But your findin's verify our gut feelin's."

"I'll write up a report." Hope took off her rubber gloves and mask. "Tomorrow I'll do a more complete autopsy and send it right to the sheriff's office."

"I appreciate that." Charlie reached out his hand to her.

"Meanwhile, keep vigilant. We want this to end before it begins." Hope squeezed Charlie's hand.

"You and me both." He elbowed Butch and they returned to the truck.

Butch slammed the door after he got in.

"Calm the hell down."

"Fuck you! If they do that to a horse, Charlie, I'll—"

"They ain't goin' to do it to a horse." Charlie backed out of the driveway. "Let's get some grub. I'm starvin'."

Butch kicked his boot into the flooring.

Charlie had to remind himself the kid was only nineteen. "All right. You calm down."

"I can't. I'm so pissed off."

"How 'bout I buy you a beer?"

"Naw. Just go back. I need to get out there tonight and look for who's doing this."

Charlie had identical thoughts. They drove back to the ranch in silence.

When he pulled up to the house, a patrol car was there. Charlie and Butch took off their hats as they entered the house, seeing Sheriff Dale Kenmore talking to Vernon. They stopped chatting when the men walked in. Vernon asked, "What did the doc say?"

"The heart's been cut out." Charlie held his hat, tired, and anxious to get out and hunt down the culprits. "She's going to do a proper check and will get you the report, Sheriff."

"We have never had this problem in these parts," Sheriff Kenmore said, "I'm not happy about it. You hear about this bullshit happening, but not up here."

Butch shifted uneasily. "Boss." He got Vernon's attention. "I'm going to do some night watch up there."

"I am too, boss." Charlie put his hat on.

"You both need to eat," Connie said, pointing to the kitchen. "Go on. Wash your hands up."

Butch headed to the kitchen, tossing his coat and hat on a chair. As he rinsed is hands at the sink, Charlie could hear the low murmur of conversation from the other room. "We'll do shifts."

"All right." Butch wiped his hands on a dish towel. He picked up a bowl and filled it with chili from the pot on the stove.

"Two hours each with the four of us. That'll cover the night."

"Good luck getting Goat up there." Butch sat down with a chunk of corn bread and began eating.

"He'll go." Charlie joined Butch at the table. "Just don't start shooting at anything that moves. All right? It ain't bear huntin' season."

"I ain't lookin for bears!"

Charlie held up his hands to calm him. "Ya can't kill people either. Just hold em, and call us. Okay?"

"Yeah."

Charlie rubbed Butch's shoulder to comfort him.

Butch looked at him and gave him a slight smile, but Charlie knew how upset this event had made Butch. It did him as well.

Chapter 3

When Charlie and Butch returned to the living room, the sheriff had left. They walked to a cabin that Butch, JP, and Goat shared and knocked. JP answered. "We need to set up a watch for a few days," Charlie said. "Butch offered to go first, two hours each. I'll take the late shift, midnight to two am. All right? You two figure out how to split the rest up."

Goat said, "Alone?"

"Take Harley," Butch said sarcastically. "You have a shotgun, Goat."

"Ya wuss." JP pushed Goat playfully.

"I'll go up the mountain after Butch," Goat said, "Then I'll wake you, Charlie."

"All right. Good," Charlie said, "Just for a few days. Then everythin' will be back to normal."

Butch and Charlie left the two men behind. "I'll do three hours, Charlie. Goat'll come knocking at your door soon enough, so get sleep now."

"You just watch yourself up there. Ya got a cell phone, use it. If there's a lot of them morons, just call and we'll get the cavalry up there. Don't be no friggin' hero."

"I know."

Charlie watched Butch walk to the barn. Ever since he had seen the mutilated deer carcass, he'd been ill at ease. That kind of thing didn't happen here. Never had.

He walked the winding path to his own cabin. Exhaustion began to hit him. The stress of not knowing what was really going on in those woods was worse than any physical exertion.

Before he closed his door to his cabin, something flew by the door. It sounded loud, like a large bird's wings. He thought about the big crow from earlier, but was too tired to dwell.

He took off his clothing, showered and went to bed.

~

A heavy knock at his door woke him. Charlie knew who it was and why. He shouted, "I'm awake, Goat. Hang a sec." He dressed quickly, putting on his heavy coat, then his hat and boots. He grabbed his cell phone and keys, opening the door to see Goat's red puffy face.

"It's fucking cold up there, Charlie. I froze my ass off."

"Did any of you see anythin'?"

"Not a fucking thing." He sighed loudly. "Fucking quiet. Seriously quiet. I didn't even hear an owl. I think we may have a one off deal, ya know?"

"Hope so. Thanks. Get some sleep." Charlie patted his back and walked to the barn while Goat headed to his cabin.

He heard the soft nickering of horses and opened Spirit's stall. "Come on, boy. I know it's late." Spirit blew out, flapping his lips at Charlie.

The chill in the air woke him up a little more. The sleepiness had left him and he felt wide awake. He saddled the horse and made sure the shotgun had twelve gauge shells loaded, but wasn't cocked.

He placed two blankets over the saddle in case the cold temperatures seeped through his jacket. With his gloves on, he hoisted himself up in the saddle and began the trail ride to the area where they had repaired the fence and found the deer.

It was crisp and clear. The dark sky was covered in stars, far more than anyone near a city could see. As he rode, his horse's hoof beats were the only sound for miles. Charlie realized Goat was right. Nothing seemed alive around him. Usually the songs of night birds or movements of nocturnal hunters were audible. Not tonight.

A chill rose to his skin, but it was under his jacket and not from the cold. He had never believed in supernatural mumbo-jumbo. Didn't pay attention to local Indian legends, and certainly never believed in ghosts.

He drew near the area where he and Butch had repaired the fence. It was intact just as they had left it.

The ground was freezing up, and Spirit's hooves snapped brittle twigs and made heavy clomps on the solid soil.

A whimper caught his attention. He stopped Spirit and listened.

A sensation stronger than chills hit him. It was borderline terror. He jumped off Spirit's back and held the reins. After a few yards, Spirit refused to keep walking with him, rearing up but not in a violent way, just being stubborn. Charlie trusted his horse's instincts. He stopped too.

Another whimper, in a very human voice, shocked him. Spirit would not move with him, so he dropped the rein and hurried towards the sound.

In the dimmest of the sliver of moonlight, Charlie found a man, naked, in the fetal position, shivering.

"Sonofabitch!" He rushed to his side and found blood spattering him. "Talk to me! Where're you hurt?" Charlie touched the man's arm.

Immediately the man's brilliant green eyes met his.

"Hang on! Hang on!" Charlie rushed back to Spirit who was looking nervous, the whites of his eyes showing. "Calm down, buddy. Don't you go crazy on me now." Charlie took a blanket off the saddle and hurried back. He wrapped it around the shivering man.

"What the hell you doin' out here in this cold? You'll get hypothermia." Charlie tried to warm him.

"F...f...freezing..."

"No wonder!" Charlie tucked the blanket closer around him. "I need to get you out of here."

"No...no police..."

"Look. I just want to get you warm, all right?"

The man nodded.

"Where's that blood comin' from?" Charlie began to check the man over. Though he was thinking only of the man's wellbeing, this guy was at least six feet tall, and built like he had weight-lifted at a gym all his life. His hair was jet black and his jaw had dark designer stubble covering it. He looked like a city boy, out of his element.

Charlie tucked the blanket high on the man's chest and inspected his legs for some kind of wound. His thighs were wide and muscular, his pubic hair was as black as the hair on his head, and the glance Charlie got of his crotch was enough to know this man was big everywhere. "Come on, partner. I got to get you warm. Can you stand?"

The man nodded, struggling to sit upright.

"You got a name?" Charlie hauled him to his feet, feeling his weight leaning heavily on him.

"Roman. Roman Burk." The man's teeth chattered.

"How on earth did you get here and why?" Charlie walked Roman to Spirit.

The horse backed up, snorting as if in fear.

"Hang on. He's all spooked." Charlie grabbed Spirit's reins and had to drag him closer. "What's with you, boy! Calm down."

The horse shifted like a nervous colt, not staying still for a second. "Spirit! Hold on. Hold on, boy." Charlie dragged Spirit closer to Roman by the chin strap, angry the horse was making a bad situation worse. "Come on, Roman. You climb on. Just step into my hands."

Roman and Spirit seemed to lock gazes. It was the oddest thing Charlie had ever seen. "Come on, Roman, he's all right."

Clinging to the blanket, Roman seemed as reluctant to get on Spirit as Spirit was for him to ride him. "Will you both calm down?" Charlie had no idea this would be an issue. He yelled at the horse, "You gonna' make me call and wake someone up? Now behave." He reached out to Roman. "Come on."

Roman moved closer.

"Climb up. I got you." Charlie cupped his hands for Roman to step into and get on the saddle.

Spirit was about to protest, but Charlie jerked his bridle to prevent it. He swung up behind Roman and put his feet into the stirrups. It took some persuading but finally Spirit began heading back down the trail.

Charlie felt Roman leaning against him, so he held him close with one arm. "Why are you up here? You know, you picked a bad time to be getting lost naked in the woods, Roman. There's some mighty odd things goin' on lately. You're lucky I found you when I did."

"Thank you."

It was so softly spoken, Charlie just caught it. Roman's hair brushed his lips as they rode back.

"Thank you, Charlie."

"I'll take care of you…" Charlie blinked. "I don't remember tellin' you my name." *Did he? He must have.*

"I know. I know you will, Charlie. You'll take good care of me."

"Have we met?" Charlie felt a strange sensation in his body.

"I'm so cold."

Charlie held him tighter. It was the best he could do with one arm. He didn't know where he was going. The hospital? Vernon's house?

"Your cabin. Please."

"Are you reading my mind?" Charlie laughed, slightly rattled.

"Please."

"You don't fret. I'll take care of you."

"Thank you, Charlie. I know you will. That's why I chose you."

Charlie imagined the cold was making Roman slightly delusional. He heard hypothermia did that. Made you hallucinate.

He rode to the barn, dismounting and helping Roman do the same. He tightened the blanket around Roman and quickly got the saddle off Spirit. Spirit was still acting like a mass of nerves, staring at Roman like Charlie had never seen him look at another human before.

He shut off the lights in the barn and held Roman around the waist as he hurried with him to his cabin. "Almost there."

"I know."

Charlie opened his door and locked it behind them. "I'll get the fire going, you go take a hot shower, ya hear me?"

Roman dropped the blanket, standing naked before him.

Charlie gulped audibly. "You...you need me to show you where everything is?"

Roman stalked him.

Charlie backed up near the fireplace. The blood spatter was in a strange pattern. Light, as if Roman had been standing beside something else that was shot or cut. But Charlie kept being drawn to Roman's eyes. The intensity of the green color, the power of his stare was hypnotic.

Roman put one hand against the cabin's exposed wooden beams over Charlie's head. He brushed his lips lightly against Charlie's.

"Sweet mother of God, I got me another gay boy." Charlie gulped and his cock went thick in his jeans.

Roman opened the buttons of Charlie's coat, pushing it off his shoulders. He took Charlie's cowboy hat off, tossing it to the sofa.

"I only had one guy, Roman. He sucked my cock back in October." Charlie stammered, "I...I don't know... I don't know if..."

Roman ran his fingers down Charlie's chest to his jeans. "If?"

"Either I'm crazy, or you are. I...I just took you off a mountain, freezing to death...you got blood all over ya."

Roman pressed his mouth against Charlie's. Charlie moaned in desire and wanted to touch Roman.

As if he knew, Roman whispered against Charlie's mouth, "Touch me."

At the invitation, Charlie wrapped his arms around Roman. "You warmed up quick. You feel like an inferno."

Roman unbuttoned Charlie's shirt, then his jeans, all the while using his tongue to explore Charlie's mouth.

I'm dreaming. I'm still sleeping and this is one helluvah dream. I knew I wanted a man. That day with Joe in the truck, well it was fate. He showed me it was what I wanted. And now I'm dreaming I found a naked beauty in the woods. Right? I'm dreaming. Wow. I don't want to wake from this one.

He heard Roman's rumbling laugh, but couldn't tell if he was reading his thoughts.

"This is *my* dream, right?"

"Yes. What do you want to do in 'your' dream?" Roman removed Charlie's shirt, smoothing his hands all over his chest.

"You're already doin' it. Is this a dream?" Charlie wasn't sure any longer.

Roman knelt in front of him, helping Charlie remove his boots, socks, jeans and briefs. When he was naked, Charlie looked at his own cock. It was stiff as a rod.

Roman enveloped it into his hot mouth.

"I like men. Oh, yessir, I like men a whole lot." Charlie widened his stance and dug his fingers through Roman's jet black hair. He glanced down to watch and when Roman opened his eyes and connected to his stare, Charlie felt his breath catch in his throat. He'd seen those eyes before. In the woods earlier.

He thought it was a wolf or a cougar. "Wow, this really is a crazy dream. I sure hope it don't turn into a nightmare and you're one of them satanic nuts."

Roman stood, holding Charlie's hand and bringing him to his bedroom. The cabin was tiny, unlike the one the other three hands shared, but Charlie preferred the privacy. It was two rooms; one open area containing a kitchen with a small table and chairs across from a sofa and love seat, and a second room with a bed and bathroom.

Roman lay down on his back and opened his legs.

Charlie stopped at the foot, staring at a man who had the most incredible body and face he had ever seen. Everything about Roman turned Charlie on. He was completely overwhelmed by lust.

Crawling from the bottom up, Charlie ran his mouth over Roman's legs as he advanced. He stared at his balls and erect cock and licked his lips. "I don't know what I want to do."

"Yes, you do." Roman gave his own dick a tug to entice.

"This is a dream, right?"

"It's anything you want it to be."

"And if I do somethin' in a dream, that don't necessarily mean it's reality."

"Suck it, Charlie."

The smile on Roman's face was ironic. Who was Charlie kidding? Dream or not, he wanted to suck this man's cock. But the odd part was, five minutes ago—or was it an hour ago?—Charlie thought he would be nursing this man back to health.

It's a dream.

He took Roman's cock into his mouth, whimpering. With the knowledge that he was indeed asleep and fantasizing, Charlie grabbed Roman's balls and felt for the first time what touching a man between his legs was like.

It's so real!

He could smell a musky scent, familiar but he didn't know why or where he had smelled it before. The taste of a dewy drop that hit his tongue was also something he felt he knew, but had no reason to recognize.

"Take me, Charlie. Fuck me."

"Why not? I can do anythin' in a dream." Charlie sat on his heels and wiped his mouth. Roman reached between Charlie's legs and rubbed something on his cock, making it slick. Charlie assumed it was spit. He never imagined bringing a gay lover here to the cabin at the ranch, so he had nothing on hand. Maybe that wasn't smart.

"Am I still dreamin'?"

"Are you?"

"I think so. I mean, none of this makes sense."

Roman gripped Charlie's cock and led it between his legs.

Charlie shivered as the head of his cock penetrated Roman's body. "That is so nice."

Roman scooted closer, so he was easily accessible to Charlie's reach. While Charlie got used to this odd dreamy sex with a man who was perfection in every way, Roman gripped Charlie's neck and dragged him down to his mouth. As Charlie kissed this perfect fantasy man, his body reacted to the extreme. He tried to pull back to gasp for air, but Roman had him in a tight grip. Charlie came, jamming his hips hard against Roman's ass. The climax was so real, Charlie figured he'd have to change the sheets from all the cum he was shooting on them.

He finally was allowed to part from the kiss. Roman jacked off, his cum spattering his chest in ribbons of white.

"My God. What a dream! I don't want to wake up." Charlie panted to catch his breath. "I can say anythin' to you, right?"

"Right." Roman swirled his index finger into the cream on his taut skin.

"You are the goddamn best lookin' man I have ever seen. I mean that. If I am imaginin' you, I have one hell of a good imagination." Charlie looked down as his cock retracted from

Roman's body. "You sure this ain't real and I shoulda' used a rubber?"

"Charlie Mosby…you are the kindest man I have ever met."

About to blush from the compliment, Charlie perked up in surprise. "Do pretend men in dreams know your last name too?"

"Men in dreams know everything."

Charlie leapt on top of Roman and rolled with him on the bed. "I don't want to wake up. *I don't want to wake up.*"

Roman's rumbling laughter was the last thing he heard before he fell asleep.

Chapter 4

"Yo! Charlie! You in there?"

Charlie bolted upright in his bed. Morning light flooded his room. He was naked and the blankets were a mess. "Be right there, Butch."

"Roman?" Charlie whispered, making sure it had been a dream and not real. The last thing he needed was to be caught with a beautiful naked man in his cabin. The teasing about his sexuality would never stop.

He hopped off the bed and looked around the tiny cabin. He was alone. Before he made his bed, he tossed back the covers, expecting a dried semen stain. Nothing.

"Never had a dream like that. Never." He washed up at the sink, splashing his face and meeting his blue eyes in the mirror. "A dream." He nodded. "No other explanation."

"Can I come in?" Butch called from outside the door.

Charlie hurried to find a pair of clean briefs and jeans, just noticing light scratches around his hips and low abdomen. He quickly tugged his zipper up and yelled back at Butch, "Come on in."

"Connie's got us some breakfast on the table." Butch stood in the living room. "You're usually first one out, but I figured you had a late night up the mountain."

"You see anythin' on your watch?" Charlie buttoned his flannel shirt and tucked it in, then sat down to put on his socks and boots.

"Nope. Maybe it was some drifters, you know? Passing through."

"So…you didn't hear or see anythin' at all?" Charlie put his coat and hat on.

"No. But that don't mean I'm not heading there first thing this morning."

"I'll talk to Vernon, but I do think we should keep an eye on that area for a while to make sure." Charlie followed Butch out of his cabin. He gave his own crotch a squeeze. Did it feel odd? Like he made love? Or…

Butch was about to say something, looking over his shoulder when he caught Charlie's movement. "Hey, maybe when Vernon's daughters get back home on break, you and me…we can take them out dancing or something."

"Huh?" Dating Vernon's daughters was the furthest thing from Charlie's mind.

"You know, Sherlane and Suzie…they're coming home from college for a bit." Butch headed up the two wooden steps to the ranch house's porch. "It's not like they'd be into Goat or JP. So I figure you and me got it easy."

"Leave Vernon's daughters alone, Butch. You're only nineteen and they're college girls, smart girls."

"When's the last time you got some pussy, Charlie?"

For some reason, the comment sounded so disrespectful to both himself and Vernon's girls that Charlie punched Butch in the face.

Butch stumbled backwards into Vernon's living room.

"Whoa! Boys!" Vernon hurried over while JP and Goat looked into the room from the kitchen where they were eating breakfast.

Butch held his jaw and glared at Charlie. "That was uncalled for, Mosby."

"You just watch your mouth, 'specially when them ladies come 'round."

Of Wolves and Men

Charlie could see Butch had caught Vernon's knowing glare. "I didn't mean nothin' by it, boss."

"You better not be referring to my girls."

Connie interrupted what was soon going to become an argument. "Come eat breakfast, boys."

Butch walked into the kitchen, still rubbing his jaw. Charlie met Vernon's gaze. "You don't worry about the girls, boss. I'll make sure no harm comes to them."

Vernon cupped Charlie's face. "You're already like a son to me and I'd never object if you were my son-in-law."

Preventing a reaction to what would never be reality, Charlie accepted the compliment gracefully. "Thank you, Vernon. But your girls can do better than me. They can marry doctors, lawyers…"

"You're the one with heart, Charlie." Vernon pounded his fist against his own chest. "You I can trust to be a good loyal husband to one of my baby girls."

Smiling shyly, Charlie tried to get out of the awkwardness. "Connie, what smells so good?"

"Pork sausages and buckwheat flapjacks. There's plenty. At least if Goat doesn't go for thirds."

Taking the plate she handed him, Charlie smiled sweetly at her. Connie and Vernon were like his mom and dad. But he knew even their kindness would evaporate if he gave any indication he did not want to be with women.

Charlie sat with his coworkers at a long wooden table with a dozen chairs surrounding it. Amid the laughter of what felt like old friends, the men finished their food and drank their coffee. Charlie didn't know what he wanted anymore. But that bizarre dream last night made him even more confused.

~

Riding Spirit, rounding up the horses that were grazing outside the paddock, Charlie galloped in the icy morning air as Butch corralled the horses from the opposite side while the hired day workers cleaned the barn. Goat and JP had spread out the hay after making sure the water wasn't frozen solid from the cold overnight temperatures.

Once the horses had been rounded up, Butch rode Scout right up to Charlie. "I'm going up the mountain."

"Want me with you?"

"I don't know. You gonna give me another punch in the jaw?"

"Get movin'." Charlie tilted his head towards the west. As he rode, he lost himself in the strange dream again. Sensual shivers covered his skin at the scent and taste of that man. The debate in Charlie's mind over how a dream could be so real was becoming obsessive.

A familiar barking noise came up behind them. Charlie laughed at Harley as he caught up to Scout to lead the way. "Go get 'em, Harley."

Charlie expected the energetic dog to do what he usually did, run to the front and sniff his way up the trail. Instead, Harley didn't pay them any attention, speeding in the direction of the damaged fence and the location of the dead doe from the day before.

"You don't think he's tracking something, do you?" Butch turned back in the saddle to ask Charlie.

"Sure looks that way. He may be a crazy dog, but he does know when somethin's up." Butch and Charlie urged their horses to keep up.

Spirit seemed to be feeling as energetic as Harley because he galloped past Scout as if they were nearing the finish line at a track.

Harley's barking intensified until Charlie figured out the dog either had something cornered, or worse, was fighting.

"If that's another dead animal I'm going to scream!" Charlie removed his shotgun, letting Spirit do the work of getting him to the dog. He cocked the gun and held it by his side.

Of Wolves and Men

An enormous black wolf appeared in a spine-tingling standoff with Harley. And fearless Harley thought he was as tough as the big lupine.

"Son of a bitch!" Charlie took a flying leap off Spirit and aimed his gun. Harley was making a clear shot impossible as he zigzagged and hopped vertically in front of the enormous timber wolf. When the wolf noticed Charlie, the green gaze of the animal's eyes made Charlie stop in his tracks. "What the hell?"

A blast of a twelve gauge sounded beside him. Butch had let off a round. The wolf leapt into the air, so high that Charlie was awestruck. Then it raced off into the dense woods. Harley gave chase but soon came back, his tongue hanging out as he panted.

Butch released the spent shell and adjusted his hat. "Well, now we know. We got ourselves a fucking wolf."

"Doc McMurray said that deer weren't killed by an animal. So it ain't no wolf. It's some person with a knife. How do you figure a wolf cut out a heart of a doe with a knife, Butch? No." He walked to where the wolf had been and knelt down to see if it left any tracks. The ground was frozen solid, so nothing was there to see.

"Well, something opened up the fence again."

Charlie spun on his heels and shook his head. "This ain't making no sense." He walked towards Butch who was inspecting the wire. "It's cut. You see? Clean cut." Charlie tugged on a piece. "That wolf had nothin' to do with this."

"Sure, Charlie. First time a wolf has been spotted 'round here, and he's got nothin' to do with killin' a doe."

"There're a few reports here and there of wolves being seen. But if he's here, it's to eat the carcass. Or maybe that was just a big ole coyote."

Butch put his shotgun back into the saddle holster. "That weren't no coyote. That wolf was at least one hundred thirty pounds. I never seen one that big." He removed a pair of pliers from the saddlebag and began working on the fence.

Charlie tried to shake off the weird feeling in his gut from the look in the animal's eyes. That connection. It felt too bizarre, like that dream he had. *Those eyes. They were Roman's eyes. But that's impossible. How could a fella you dreamed have the same set of eyes as a wolf?*

"You goin' to help me, or stand there starin' at the trees?"

Charlie snapped into focus and knelt beside Butch to reconnect the cut wires. "We better look around for a dead animal before we go."

"Yeah. My thoughts too." Butch said to Harley, "Hey, dog. Go find us another dead deer. Make yourself useful."

Harley ignored him, sniffing and marking his territory.

The damage to the fence was minor compared to the previous night. They were able to reconnect the cut wires without having to patch it. While Butch put the tools away, Charlie mounted Spirit and took a ride around the area to see if he could find anything amiss.

He walked the horse in the direction the wolf had been. Charlie looked down at Harley as he sniffed the frozen ground. There were blood stains, or at least it appeared to be blood. Charlie hopped off and knelt down near the dog. He touched the brown color and looked at the tip of his finger. In the icy morning, nothing should be wet. "You hit that wolf, Butch."

"Naw. How could I hit it? It just ran away like nothin' was wrong."

Charlie glanced up at Butch who was atop Scout. He showed him his reddish fingertip. "I think ya nicked him."

"Shoulda' killed him."

Charlie stood beside Scout, leaning on the horse's neck. "Don't be killin' wolves just because you don't like 'em."

"They're considered pests. I can shoot 'em."

"They're not pests." Charlie pointed at Harley. "You wouldn't have him without that 'pest'."

Of Wolves and Men

"So you'd rather have wolves feedin' on and killin' our ponies? What has gotten into you lately? I swear, I thought we were alike when I first met you. But the more I know you, the less alike we are."

"Are you stupid? Were you at the doc's when she told us it weren't no animal that killed that doe? And you think somethin's gotten into me?" Charlie walked back to Spirit, whose ears were perked as if he were listening to their argument.

"I'm headin' back to the ranch." Butch spun Scout around and started walking the pinto down the trail. Harley raced to lead the way back.

Charlie petted Spirit and watched Butch vanish around tall trees. He shook his head and swung his leg over the saddle, picking up the reins. "Ya think ya know a man, Spirit, then ya don't."

Spirit answered with a snort into the cold air.

Charlie wandered the perimeter of Vernon's property line. He paused to look out over the reservoir. Its serenity reflected the blue sky.

"*Charlie.*"

Charlie jumped out of his skin and looked for the origin of the soft whisper that he could have sworn said his name. He tugged the reins and made Spirit turn in a complete circle.

"I'm goin' nutty." Charlie was about to head back to the ranch when he heard it again. He tapped his heels against Spirit to make him walk towards the sound, but Spirit began resisting.

"What's wrong, boy? Go." Charlie squeezed his knees, trying to get the horse to move.

Spirit shifted his weight side to side to intentionally avoid going where Charlie wanted him to. The more Charlie asked him to obey, the more upset Spirit became. "What is with you?" Charlie backed him up, turned him in another direction and had no problem. He made a wide circle and tried to again go towards where he had heard the whisper. Spirit reared and made a noise of fear.

That was enough to make Charlie a believer. He dismounted and held the reins, taking slow steps towards a stand of evergreens. Spirit protested loudly and dug in his hooves. Charlie wished Harley had stuck around. "Fine." He brought the horse in the opposite direction and tied him to a tree to make sure he didn't bolt from whatever was scaring him. And something was. Charlie removed the shotgun but didn't chamber a round.

He walked towards the darkness of the trees and strained to see into the thickness of the low hanging branches.

"Charlie."

His jaw dropping in shock, Charlie said, "I cannot believe my eyes! Now, you can't tell me I'm dreamin' in the middle of the mornin'." He set the shotgun aside and knelt next to Roman, who was once again naked and shivering. This time Roman was holding his shoulder, blood seeping through his fingers.

"Don't you own any clothes?" He took off his sheepskin-lined coat and covered Roman. "What did you do this time?" Charlie nudged back Roman's hand to see what looked to be a graze of a one of the shotgun round's pellets. The skin was sliced and beginning to get red and angry. "Hang on. I got a first aid kit on the saddle."

As Charlie walked to Spirit, who was not looking comfortable at all at the moment, he tried to make sense of this strange man. "If that weren't no dream, then I…" Charlie removed a small box from a saddlebag. *Did I make love to you last night?*

Charlie looked over his shoulder, half-expecting Roman to not be there when he checked.

He returned with his kit and knelt down beside him. "I'm at a loss, Roman. Are you some kind of naturist who don't believe in clothing?" He dabbed at the wound, making Roman hiss like a cat as he flinched from the sting. "This time of year, ya have to wear clothes. I swear, I don't know who's crazier. Me for thinkin' you're real, or you for being so stupid." He used gauze and white tape to patch up the wound. "There. I suppose you need me to take you back to my place and borrow clothing."

Roman lunged at him, connecting their mouths, gripping Charlie's shoulders.

Charlie blinked and braced himself before he was slammed into the trunk of the trees they were under. He broke the kiss and gasped at Roman. "What are you?" He stared into the depth of Roman's eyes, and the green gaze made his skin prickle with warning. "I did make love you last night, didn't I? You kept tellin' me I was dreamin' but—"

Roman tackled Charlie and pinned him to the ground, devouring his mouth and grinding his cock on Charlie's crotch.

Charlie was sure someone had tainted the water on the ranch. There was no mistaking he was awake, but how he kept finding this naked man who had an insatiable appetite for sex was confusing the heck out of him.

With an effort Charlie turned away from the hungry kisses. "Hold on, Roman...hang on!" Charlie felt Roman opening his shirt, the jacket had slid off Roman's body and the sight of his sculpted biceps and rounded chest muscles was beginning to get Charlie into that state he was in last night. Pure lust, aching to hump. "What's going on? How does a man end up naked on this mountain? Especially a gay one who looks like a city boy. Come on, Roman. You and I had unprotected sex last night. I feel slightly violated now. You knew I was out of it, thinkin' it wasn't real."

"It's not real now." Roman smiled and his pure white teeth made him appear wicked.

Charlie didn't know what to say. What do you say to a naked Greek god who's hot for your cock?

While Charlie's heart felt as if it were exploding in his chest, Roman opened his jeans and hunted for his prick. He grasped Charlie's cock and exposed it from his clothing. After Roman admired it, smoothed his hands over the length, he sank his dick into his mouth, nearly to the base.

Charlie arched his back and closed his eyes at the rush. Questions were spinning in his head. *Who are you? What are you? Where did you come from? Why me?*

But all those thoughts were gone as his body began to rise. "Roman…Jesus! I thought Joe knew how to suck cock!" Charlie grabbed the dirt under him, digging his nails into it as the intensity began to turn his body into pure pleasure.

Roman was drawing hard suction while holding tightly with his hand. He engulfed his cock deep, then nearly allowed it to slip out of his lips. Charlie fucked him orally, going wild as Roman used his tongue to swirl around his cock while it was still inside his hot, wet mouth.

The intensity was too much for Charlie. Going from nothing but masturbating, and that rarely, to incredible head, made Charlie want to come, not edge the climax.

He threw back his head and clenched his teeth as he came. The orgasm was so strong, he could barely exhale or open his eyes. His body rocked and his cock pulsated as Roman moaned, or purred? The sound was cat-like…or wolf-like? Charlie was too high from the pleasure swoon to think.

When Roman had milked Charlie for all he could give, licking the drops from his slit, Roman knelt up and reached his hands over his head in a strange gesture. Victory? Joy?

Charlie blinked and tried to recuperate. He gazed from Roman's dark five o'clock shadow down his chest to his engorged cock. It was thick, red, and veins showed through the skin, it was so hard.

Lunging at him, Charlie used both hands to push Roman backwards to the ground. At first Roman let out a snarl in anger, but when Charlie gripped the base of that formidable cock and enveloped it into his mouth, that growl of defense quickly changed to a purr.

Inhaling his musky scent, Charlie sucked Roman with the same intensity Roman had sucked him. *I want to swallow. Come in my mouth, you fucking wild beast!*

A low rumbling sound came from Roman's chest as if he were amused, or laughing. Charlie didn't care if he could read his mind.

Suddenly Roman gripped Charlie's head and began orally fucking him. Charlie wasn't prepared for that. It was only the second time he'd had a cock in his mouth, and the first one was barely a taste.

He tried to back off, pushing Roman's hips before he embarrassed himself and gagged. But prior to that happening, Roman came.

Charlie didn't know what to do because Roman's grip on him made moving away impossible. He swallowed the load before he had a chance to think about it. *Well, I did tell myself I would.* Roman pumped into his mouth again. More cum hit the back of Charlie's tongue. Down it went as well. When Roman's cock stopped throbbing, he released his hold on Charlie's head.

Charlie leaned on his elbow, wiping his mouth. "What are you? Some kind of animal? Christ, I told you I'm new at this. Ya could have let me set the pace."

Then Roman jolted in fear so powerfully under him that Charlie gasped and leapt back. Roman spun around, staring behind him as if something terrorized him.

"What?" Charlie said, trying to close his pants and shirt. "Roman? What? Do you see a wolf?"

Roman jumped to his feet and vanished into the woods.

"Wait! Let me help you!" Charlie rose to his feet clumsily, tucking in his shirt and rushing to see where Roman had gone. Spirit was snorting and stomping in mortal fear.

"Roman! Don't fight it alone!" Charlie grabbed his jacket from the ground, putting it on, then he picked up his shotgun. He raced in the direction he thought Roman had gone but he was nowhere to be seen. "Roman!" Charlie called, feeling empty and alone. "Roman! Let me help you!" When he felt his eyes sting with tears, Charlie grew angry at himself. He swore under his breath at getting involved with a wild-man, then picked up the first aid kit, returning it and his shotgun to the saddle.

"You're not helpin' me any!" he yelled at Spirit who was spinning like a top from nerves. "Just calm down. All right? There ain't nuthin' here."

Charlie swung his leg up and over the saddle. Before he left, he noticed a big black crow perched on a birch tree branch. Below it was what looked like a piece of white gauze, lying on the ground.

"I give up. That man is nuttier than a fruitcake." He turned Spirit in the direction of the ranch and rode down the trail. "I have got to stop goin' near him. That fella does not have all his marbles." Charlie shook his head. "I'd be better off lookin' for Joe and takin' my chances with a man like that, then tryin' to deal with a macho-fella who's half nuts."

The closer they got to the ranch, the calmer Spirit became. But Charlie was a mess. The sexual contact with Roman was ideal, but nothing about that man made sense.

Chapter 5

Before he even made it to the barn, Charlie heard a young woman's squeal of joy and spotted a yellow Ford Escort parked near the ranch house.

Sherlane was obviously just arriving home from college.

Charlie's mind was so confused at the moment, he was struggling to function and do things he had done over and over again, like get Spirit out of his saddle and bridle.

The conversation right outside the barn was nothing but noise. Charlie couldn't make any of it out, but it was obvious the other boys were as excited to see Vernon's daughter as Connie and Vernon were.

Charlie put Spirit's halter on, and led him to the paddock where the other horses were grazing on piles of hay.

"Go on, ya pain in the butt." Charlie slapped Spirit's rump and he trotted happily towards his equine friends.

Just as he closed the gate, Sherlane jumped into his arms in greeting. "Charlie Mosby! You just get cuter and cuter every time I visit!"

The brown-eyed brunette nearly knocked his cowboy hat off in her excitement. He grabbed it and held on. "Howdy, Sherlane." He noticed her parents and the other three men watching. Butch was the only one with a jealous spark in his eye.

He backed away from her politely and brushed off his hands, trying to not offend her. "I was just up the mountain...sorry."

"Don't be." She grinned flirtatiously.

"Come on," Connie waved at her as she hollered, "let's all have some lunch. Suzie should be here any minute."

Sherlane reached for Charlie's hand as if to escort him to the house with her.

"Hun, I have to stop at the cabin and wash up. I'll be there in a bit."

"Don't be long." She batted her lashes over her shoulder as she walked with the others.

Charlie looked down at his boots, wondering if he had the scent of a man's groin all over him. It felt that way, but maybe the aroma of horse was stronger.

He didn't even glance at the rest of the group as he walked the path to his cabin. Standing in the living room, Charlie took off his coat, intent on a shower and change of clothing. He stood by the foot of his bed, removing his boots and unzipping his jeans. Something hit the window. Loudly.

He started in surprise and looked out of the blinds. Nothing was there. Shaking it off, he continued to undress, planning to tell Butch he had no reason to feel jealous because…

Another loud bang shook him up. He tugged the cord, lifting the blinds all the way up. There was shrubbery around his cabin, bare from the coming winter. Just as he was about to drop the blinds, a large bird hit the glass.

"What the fuck?" Charlie leaned against the window sill to see. That crow, or one that looked exactly like it, was perched on a tree branch and making diving hits at Charlie's window. "Stop! Are you crazy, ya dumb bird? It's a window! You'll knock yourself out!" He straightened his back. "Now I'm talkin' to birds." Shaking his head as if he knew he was insane, Charlie lowered the shade and continued to head to the shower. Another thump, louder than the two before, hit the glass. "He's goin' to break the damn thing."

Intending to go around the side of his cabin and chase the bird away, Charlie opened the front door and the bird flew over his head into the room, scaring him to death. He spun around, expecting to be pecked in the face. Instead he found Roman Burk sitting naked on his floor, catching his breath.

Charlie choked in shock and quickly shut and locked his door. "Now hang on..."

"Don't go with Sherlane or Suzie. Please."

Charlie hurried to the window and looked out. "Please tell me that you aren't that crazy bird."

"Charlie...I need you!"

"How the heck? Look. Are you puttin' LSD into my drinking water?" Charlie knew he was not right in the head. "Did you see a big crow fly in here? Or am I desperately in need of a doctor?"

Roman struggled to get to his feet. Charlie could see his legs shaking. "Buddy, you seriously need to stop runnin' around like a madman. You sprinted so fast after what we did up the mountain I thought...well, I don't know what I thought." Charlie scratched his head. "I don't know what to think at all."

Roman seemed to struggle to walk, to close the small gap between them. He hung his arms over Charlie's shoulders and shifted all his weight onto Charlie for support. "Don't go with either of them. Please."

Charlie struggled to hold Roman up. He was a big man. "Look, here...Roman, I have no intention of goin' with either of Vernon's daughters. But, how did you get in here? I mean it. I don't believe in paranormal bullshit, but I swear a crow just flew in here, and then there you are again, naked as a jaybird."

"Don't go with them. Don't go with them."

"I should get you some help. I don't mean any offense, Roman, but somethin' ain't right."

Roman leaned back, staring into Charlie's eyes.

Charlie not only melted from the need in them, he grew hard. Shaking his head, Charlie said softly, "What you do to me...the way you excite me, well...it's a crime."

"It is a crime. It *was* a crime."

"I meant that as a joke. Bein' gay ain't illegal."

"No. No. What they did to me. *What they did to me!*"

Charlie's cell phone rang. "Crud. That'll be the gang wonderin' why I'm not up there eatin' lunch. You're goin' to get me into hot water."

"Charlie…I need you."

The pain in Roman's eyes tore Charlie apart. He tried to get him to stand on his own, accidentally brushing Roman's shoulder with the fresh wound on it. He noticed the gauze was gone. "Sit."

Roman did, reluctantly, reaching to touch Charlie's fingers as Charlie took his phone out of his jacket pocket.

"Hello?"

"What's taking so long?"

"Sherlane, I'm tuckered out. I'm goin' to just rest a bit."

"No. Come on, Charlie. You have to eat lunch. And Suzie is here. She wants to say hello."

Charlie gazed down at Roman's eyes. "No. And don't come here neither. I need some shut eye. I'll see you'all at dinner."

"Charlie," she whined.

"You just stay with your mom and dad." Charlie toyed with Roman's fingers. "They miss you most."

"Suzie will be disappointed."

"She'll live. Let me rest. Bye." Charlie shut off the phone. He set it on the side table and stared at Roman.

Roman held Charlie by his hips and brought him to stand between his knees.

"I don't get answers from you, Roman. But your appetite for sex is another question I have. Are you what they call a nympho?"

"It's called a satyriasis if you're male." Roman kissed Charlie's zipper flap. "And yes. I am now."

"Are 'now'." Charlie ran his hands over his own head in confusion. "What were you before?"

"An ATF agent."

Of Wolves and Men

Charlie tried to back up, but Roman had him in a firm hold. "Okay, what mental hospital did you escape from? You really are a mess, buddy."

"A mess you want, Charlie." Roman began chewing on Charlie's cock through his jeans.

His length pulsating in the grasp of Roman's teeth, Charlie asked, "What's an ATF agent doin' up in these parts?"

"Talk later."

His cock was exposed from his clothing, and immediately sucked deeply.

Charlie began to swoon from the sensation. He held onto Roman by his shoulders. "You say talk later, but you'll fly out of here the way you flew in." Charlie kept quiet to enjoy the oral sex then asked, "Did you fly in here?"

Roman ignored him, drawing him deeper into his mouth, holding Charlie's hips and pulling and pushing him in and out.

"My Lord what have I gotten myself into?" Charlie looked up at the ceiling fan as he was serviced by an ATF agent. *An ATF agent? No way. An out-patient more like.*

He felt his clothing being dragged down his legs. Charlie stepped out of it, while Roman helped, one leg at a time. When he was naked, Roman tackled Charlie roughly, pinning him to the throw rug in front of the hearth. Charlie had no complaints. He loved roughhousing. Perfect foreplay.

They grappled, wrestling on the floor, laughing yet still battling for dominance. When Roman pinned him down on his back, he looked like a wild wolf controlling a competing male from the pack. The smile dropped from Charlie's face as he caught his bright green gaze. One he recognized now.

"Hang on a minute." A strange tingling sensation covered Charlie's skin. The memory of the sound of Butch's shotgun, the black timber wolf jumping and escaping, the wound to Roman's shoulder…a graze of one of the spread-pattern's pellets.

Roman showed his teeth in a sensual snarl that sent the hairs rising on Charlie's neck. He was tossed to his stomach, his hips raised into the air roughly, and fucked. Hard.

"Sweet Jesus!" Charlie braced himself, cringing and trying to break free. "Roman! Stop! What are you doing?" Charlie could not get out of the powerful grip and didn't know if this was a rape or consensual.

I want this. I just want this safe!

"Roman. Have a heart! Christ Almighty!"

A growl, not a human voice, but a wolf's growl filled Charlie's ears. He froze under Roman as Roman humped him. Charlie was afraid to look. His skin was being scratched by sharp nails.

"Roman!" Charlie cringed as the sex became carnal in nature. He felt Roman's cock throbbing inside him and held his breath in apprehension, staying perfectly still. He had no idea if this was how gay sex should be. Painful. Rough. And risky.

Then Charlie felt nothing at all. Cold air. He spun around and found his cabin door open, and the sight of a furry black pair of hind legs and fluffy tail vanishing out of it.

He gasped in astonishment, his brain trying to catch up with his vision. On his hands and knees, Charlie crawled to the door and slammed it shut, struggling to reach the knob, locking it, terrified someone would see him in this state.

Shaking, frightened that he was either was losing his mind, or something strange was in his blood, like he accidentally ingested peyote mushrooms or another hallucinogenic, Charlie stumbled to the bathroom. He turned on the light and looked at his back and ass in the mirror over the sink. He was scratched up and red, like a cougar had fought him.

Leaning his palms on the sink, he tried to think. But every thought he had was upside down and backwards.

Of Wolves and Men

Barely functioning, Charlie turned the water on in the shower and touched his bottom. He was sore and becoming angry. He entered the tub, allowing the water to calm and soothe him. The more he thought about it, the more furious he became. And the worst part was the images...a crow hitting his window, flying inside his cabin. *Changing into Roman? Can't be.*

Then Roman having sex with him. A strange growling sound. The sensations changing. Seeing a wolf leave?

"I have been raped by a wolf." He laughed. "Sure, Charlie. Tell that to a shrink and you'll be in a rubber room for life."

~

By six in the evening, Charlie was lying on his sofa staring into space. He had work to do. Oh yes. Plenty. He just couldn't leave the cabin right now.

A light knock sounded at his door.

"Oh no." Charlie rubbed his face in exhaustion. "I'm not feeling well," he yelled, trying to be heard.

Suzie's voice replied, "I have your dinner, Charlie. You have to eat."

He looked down at his stocking feet and jeans. After letting go of a big, exhaled sigh, he managed to get off the sofa and open the door.

Freshman college student Suzie Norman was a petite, blue-eyed blonde ex-cheerleader from Wasatch High. He could just about see her shaking her gold and black pompoms on the football field, yelling, "Go Wasps!"

"Charlie Mosby...look at you." She set an aluminum foil wrapped plate on the coffee table and embraced him like she was his long-lost girlfriend.

He winced as she rubbed a raw spot on his back but hid it behind clenched teeth. Parting from her, he asked, "So? How's college?"

"We can catch up while you eat. Come on, handsome." She picked up the plate and set it on the small table, unwrapping it. "Pork chops, hash, and Mom's apple pie."

Charlie sat at the table as she hurried to get a fork and knife from a drawer in the kitchen, opening the fridge. "I knew I should have brought you a cold one. Butch said you always have some, but you don't."

"I'm all right."

Suzie gave him the utensils and a glass of juice, then she sat down. She leaned her jaw on her palm, staring at him.

He tasted the food. "Mm. I was hungry."

"How're you feeling now? You still tired?"

"A little. I'm all right. Been some crazy things goin' on lately."

"I heard about the deer. Oh, Charlie, that is so scary. But Butch and Goat said nothing's happened since then. Are you going back up to watch again tonight?" She leaned closer. "I can go with you."

A bang was heard on his window.

Suzie jumped out of her skin and spun around.

Charlie grumbled. "There's a crow that keeps flyin' into my window. Ignore it."

"How bizarre!"

"I think it's confused." He kept eating.

"Anyway, like I said, if you want, I can saddle Petunia up and we can ride up the mountain. It's cold, but it's a beautiful night."

Another bang came from the glass.

"You sure that's a bird?" She shivered visibly.

"Yeah. Hang on." Charlie walked to the window and peeked out of the blind. The crow was tilting its head at him. "You behave!" Charlie wagged his finger.

Suzie laughed. "You are a real riot, Charlie. Telling a bird to behave itself. I never met a fella like you."

Charlie made eye contact with the crow. He gave it a scolding glance. If it was Roman, he'd better stop what he was doing.

Of Wolves and Men

He felt Suzie standing behind him. She leaned against him to look outside. "You always feel and smell so nice, Charlie."

Her breasts pressed against his back. Just as Charlie was about to step away from the window, a large black wolf with its canines bared began biting at the glass.

Suzie screamed and jumped backwards, so terrified she nearly knocked over the kitchen table and chairs.

"Stay there." Charlie pointed to her.

"You can't go out there! Charlie! There hasn't been wolves out here forever. He's got to be rabid biting at a window. Where's your shotgun?"

"I said stay here! Ya got me? It ain't a wolf. Okay?"

"Ain't a wolf? I saw that thing with my own eyes!"

"Are you gonna listen to me?"

"Yes, Charlie." She bit her nail and wrapped her arms tightly across her chest.

Charlie stormed outside and walked to the side of the cabin. Roman was standing behind the shrubs, naked of course.

"Don't you go with her," Roman said, looking ragged.

"Go away!" Charlie looked over his shoulder. "You're causin' more trouble, bitin' like a rabid hound at my window."

"Charlie...promise me."

"Promise you?" Charlie tried to shout and keep his voice low at the same time. "You fucked me like a damn dog in there!" He pointed to the cabin. "Don't you do that again!"

"Never. I...I sometimes... I sometimes..."

"Go. Shoo. She'll see you and I'll be in trouble."

"Charlie...don't sleep with her."

"I ain't interested in women!" Charlie stopped short. "My God. Did I just say that?"

"Charlie? You okay?" Suzie called from the door.

"Charlie...I need you. Please."

"I hear ya. I do. But if someone finds out..." Charlie looked over his shoulder. "Now I'm beggin' *you*, Roman."

"Anything. Yes."

"Now, go buy yourself some clothing. Fer cryin' out loud." Charlie shook his head and returned to the cabin.

Suzie stood in the open doorway. "Is it still there?"

"It's just a feral dog. I shooed him away. Hey, Suzie, I am real tired. Can I just be alone?"

"Sure, Charlie." She looked rejected.

"I'll be certain to spend time with you'all tomorrow. Just not tonight. I'm feelin' out of sorts. Okay?"

"Okay."

She made a move as if she were going to kiss him. A loud flapping noise and a gust of air made her jerk back and wave over her head.

Charlie rolled his eyes. "It's just a bat. See ya tomorrow, Suzie."

Suzie scooted off in a hurry, ducking as if bats would get tangled in her hair. Charlie shut the door and found Roman sitting at the table eating his dinner.

"I guess you're hungry, Mr. Burk. Mr. Crow or whatever you decide to be today."

"Starved."

He sat down across from Roman and stared at him. Roman took a bite, then fed Charlie, sharing the meal.

"What have I gotten myself into?" Charlie sighed.

"You?" Roman laughed. "I got news for you, friend. You don't have near the trouble I'm in at the moment."

"I'm getting that feelin'."

"You have no idea." Roman fed him another bite of pork chop.

Charlie stared at the handsome man and let out another loud sigh.

Chapter 6

When Roman picked up the empty dinner plate and began licking it, Charlie slumped back in his chair and gaped at him. "You're actin' like Harley."

Roman lowered the dish and said, "That dog is a pain in the ass." He used his forearm to wipe his face until Charlie handed him a paper napkin.

"Roman, what are you? Are you one of them orphans brought up by wolves? I swear, you give me the creeps sometimes..." Charlie met Roman's intense gaze. "Most of the time."

"Babe, you have no idea what I have been dealing with. I was seriously in the wrong place at the wrong time."

A knock sounded at the cabin door. "Charlie, you in there?"

"It's Butch. You have got to make yourself scarce." Charlie stood. "Shoo. Fly. Or go hide under the bed. But be quiet."

"Charlie?" Butch called, knocking louder.

Roman's lip curled in a snarl. "He shot me."

"He shot at a wolf, not you. Go." Charlie held Roman's forearm and urged him to go into the bedroom.

"You want to fuck him, don't you?" Roman was being stubborn.

"No!" Charlie lowered his voice. "You are one possessive critter, you know that? Now do you want to expose me as a queer? I'm not ready for that. Okay?" Charlie shook his head at Roman. "Goddamn naked man-hunk in my cabin. What do you think Butch'll think about that?"

"Man-hunk?" Roman got a look of lust in his eyes.

"Charlie Mosby? You open this door!"

"Keep yer boots on!" Charlie yelled at Butch. "Let me get rid of him."

Roman rubbed the sore wound on his shoulder, glaring at the door Butch was behind. Finally he relented and went into the bedroom. Charlie closed the door, straightened his shirt and ran his hand through his hair. He opened the door, but not all the way, keeping his foot wedged against it, preventing it from moving. "What."

"Vernon asked me to check on you. I want to take the girls out dancing but they won't come without you."

"Take Goat. I'm not goin'."

"Take Goat? Did you just tell me to take Goat?" Butch pushed on the door.

Charlie held it in place. "Look, I'm not goin' out tonight. I'm not feelin' right and if I go anywhere, it'll be back up the mountain to check on the fence."

"I just got back from there." Butch shoved at the door harder. "Why aren't you lettin' me in?"

Charlie glanced behind him and opened the door with reluctance.

"Mosby, there's something seriously wrong with you." Butch took off his cowboy hat and sat on a chair. "There are two pretty gals up at the house, dying for some fun time on their college break."

"You ain't even old enough to drink."

"No one checks at the Other Side Tavern. You and I have been there together drinking, so you know that." Butch rose to his feet and came within an inch of Charlie's nose, suspicion written all over him. "You better come clean, Mosby. What the hell's really going on?"

Charlie heard a low growl coming from the bedroom. Butch must have as well, because he perked up and stared at the closed door.

"You best be goin'." Charlie began to lead Butch out.

"You didn't even ask me what I found up the mountain. Do you even care about the ponies anymore? Or has everything sane been lost on you?" Butch jerked out of Charlie's grip.

"Sorry. What did you find?"

"Wires cut again."

"Seriously?"

"Yeah. But I didn't find no dead animal."

"Did you fix it?"

"Course I did."

"I'll head up there now." Charlie picked up his coat and hat.

"What am I supposed to tell the girls?" Butch stepped outside when Charlie opened the door.

"Tell 'em I'm busy. And take Goat or JP."

The minute Charlie stood with his back at the open door, an enormous black crow flew out of the living room making both men duck and shout out in fright.

Charlie swallowed his nerves while Butch gaped in astonishment. "Did that thing just fly out of your cabin?"

"It's been hangin' around, hittin' the window. I think maybe it's stunned or somethin'." Charlie shut the door behind him.

"You tellin' me that thing was inside your place?"

"No. I don't know." Charlie looked around the area, keeping them both headed in the direction of the ranch house. He could see a dark shadow trailing them. *What are you doing, Roman? If Butch catches sight of you like that, he'll kill you! Just what we need. A huge black wolf living at the ranch. Lord have mercy.*

"Stop pushing me." Butch jerked his shoulder away from Charlie's constant nudging. "You're lucky when you punched my jaw I didn't hit you back."

"Ooh, I'm so scared," Charlie teased, laughing.

That appeared to anger Butch. He stopped short and wheeled around on his boot heels to face Charlie, his finger pointing into Charlie's face. "Don't make me kick your ass."

"Look here, Crowell." Charlie poked him in the chest. "I'm the boss of you. You got that? I got six years of life experience more than you. *You got that?*" He poked him harder. "An' I'm not real happy with you either lately. Talkin' trash about Vernon's daughters, givin' me lip constantly. You just watch yourself."

A deep low snarl was heard distinctly by both men. Charlie rolled his eyes while Butch nearly jolted out of his boots. "Somethin's out here, Charlie."

"Nothin' is. Go inside." Charlie persuaded Butch to keep walking to the ranch house. When he opened the door, both girls were dressed to go out to the tavern, holding their purses and wearing their coats.

"Charlie!" Sherlane rushed towards him. "You are coming to the tavern for a drink, right?"

"No. I'm headed up the mountain. Sorry."

Suzie nudged her sister out of the way. "Dad won't let us go if you're not there." She glanced at Butch in annoyance. "So if you don't go, we can't."

"Take Goat or JP. They're great for chaperones and they'll keep this wolf off you." Charlie gestured to Butch.

"Speaking of wolves…" Suzie's eyes widened. "While I was at Charlie's cabin a big wolf-like dog bit at the window."

Charlie tried to stem the tide of information before it instilled a panic. "No. I told you it was just a feral dog. Don't go spreadin'—"

Harley bolted out of the open ranch house door, barking like he was about to kill something.

Butch pushed Charlie out of the way and rushed after the dog. "Get the shotgun, Charlie! I told ya somethin' was out here!"

"Shit!" Charlie could see Vernon and Connie becoming aware something was going on. "Go inside, girls. It's nothin'. I told you it's just a lost doggie. Okay?"

Of Wolves and Men

"Charlie," Suzie pouted as she spoke. "Be real careful. He was a big ole dog."

He sprinted, trying to catch Butch and Harley. To his anguish, he found them all inside the open horse paddock. The horses were going crazy, rearing, making whining noises of fear and stampeding to and fro.

It was dark but for two spotlights attached high on the barn. Harley's barking was keeping Charlie on target as to where the chaos was. When he spotted Butch with a shotgun Charlie gasped. "No!"

"Harley! Clear them horses back!" Butch chambered a round with a 'cha-chunk' sound and brought the shotgun up to aim.

Charlie grabbed the gun by the barrel and a blast of buckshot hit the dirt in front of them, blowing a hole in the ground and spattering dried mud into their faces. The horses went berserk at the blast.

As Charlie fought Butch for the gun, Vernon and the rest of the family finally caught up to the action.

"There's a big black wolf in the horse paddock, Charlie! What the hell are you doing?" Butch yelled.

"You'll hit the horses! You know the spread pattern on that thing? Are you nuts?" He jerked the gun away and removed the cartridges.

"He's the nut, boss!" Butch pointed at Charlie, catching his breath. "There's a huge timber wolf inside this paddock. I bet you that's what's doing all the weird killing."

"Harley!" Vernon called and heard the dog yelp in pain.

"Roman!" Charlie jumped the paddock fence and scattered the already panicked horses. He spotted Roman, naked, crawling under the far side of the wooden fence in the dark.

Hearing footsteps behind him, Charlie stopped and spun around. He held up his hands. "It's gone."

"Where's Harley?" Vernon looked for the dog.

He was wagging as he approached Vernon. Vernon picked the dog up to inspect him and got a lick in the face. "You're all right, little buddy." Vernon held him in one arm. "Who the hell is Roman?"

Charlie choked, not realizing he had actually called his name out loud. "Uh. Who?"

Butch folded his arms over his chest. "Yeah, Charlie. Who's Roman? That your new dog who's terrorizing everything?"

"I don't have a new dog." Charlie tried to see out into the darkness. "Why don't you let me check on the horses and do my job?" When Butch just stared at him, Charlie said, "Go get Goat and JP. Let's just make sure the horses are all right, then get them inside for the night. Can you do that, Butch?"

Vernon said, "All right, boys. Calm down. Butch, do as the man says."

Connie touched her daughters on the shoulders. "Come on. Back inside. There ain't no one going out on the town tonight. There's too much insanity going on right now."

Suzie gave Charlie her puppy-dog eyes but he turned away. He walked into the group of horses to see if anyone of them had been hurt. They were slow to calm down after being frightened. One by one, Charlie led them by the halter to Vernon, who walked them into the barn.

"*Charlie!*"

Charlie ground his jaw and looked over his shoulder to make sure no one was around before meeting up with Roman. "You have any idea the trouble you're causin' me?"

"You think I have any control over this bullshit?" Roman shivered, rubbing his arms. "And that stupid dog is the problem. Not me."

"You're not the one killin' them deer up the mountain, are you?" Charlie could see Vernon walking closer to get another horse to inspect in the light. "Go wait at my cabin. I got to check all these horses out and get them in the stables."

"They're fine. I didn't touch them."

Of Wolves and Men

"Go."

Charlie brought another two horses over to Vernon, seeing the other three men coming over to help out. "Boss, none of them are hurt. Harley just shook 'em up."

"No harm in making sure. And they're used to Harley's antics. No. The dog had something." He took another two horses by the halter and walked them to the barn.

JP asked, "What's the plan, Charlie?"

"Just look 'em over in the light. Make sure they didn't hurt themselves. Then put them in their stalls for the night."

JP and Goat immediately complied. Butch asked, "Who's Roman?"

"There ain't no Roman. Now go help out before I get mad."

Butch entered the enclosed area and walked two more horses out. Charlie rubbed his face in frustration. He had no idea what to do about Roman.

~

Roman paced inside Charlie's cabin. He felt pent up and caged. Dragging his fingers through his hair, he clenched his teeth, Roman didn't want to mess up Charlie's life. But he needed help. And Charlie was the one to help him. He just felt it in his gut.

Roman looked down at his hands. He was filthy. Something he was getting used to. It had never been that way. He was a well groomed man before this happened to him. Figuring Charlie was going to be a while checking out a herd of horses that size, he stood in front of the bathroom mirror and stared at himself. It wasn't often he could see his reflection anymore. He didn't exactly live in his city apartment any longer.

He rubbed his hands over the scruffy black stubble on his jaw and looked at his teeth. "Fuck!" He looked like a wild animal more every day. He reached into the tub, turning on the shower. When was the last time he'd had a hot scrub down? Cold water dipping into streams and lakes, yes. That was his new bath time. Not fun. No. Not fun at all.

He stepped under the running water, moaning in pleasure. Using Charlie's soap and shampoo, he washed himself over and over, as if he could rinse off the curse he was saddled with. He leaned both hands on the shower wall, letting the hot water run over him, knowing a hot scrub wasn't going to happen often. His cock became hard and a shiver washed up his spine. "No." He shut the water, standing still, dripping. "No!"

The first place he felt it was his teeth. Always his teeth. Then his cock. He stepped out of the tub and wiped the steam off the mirror, inspecting his mouth. His canines grew longer. Through the misty fog of the hot steam, a figure appeared in the mirror behind him. A hideous red mask of a painted woman. "It wasn't me!" Roman spun around to nothing. He screamed into the echoing wet room, "I wasn't the one who arranged the search. Why me? Why do this to me?"

He covered his face and slid down a wall to the corner, shivering and knowing he could not battle this curse that was sent upon him. He simply didn't know how.

~

It was late and he was dead on his feet. Charlie had had intentions of going out to check the fence line but not after having to inspect sixty-five horses.

He opened his cabin door, taking off his coat and hat. "Roman? You here or did you fly out the door again?" He poked his head into the bedroom and noticed a light coming from under the bathroom door. "You all right?"

A low growl followed by scratching of wood alerted Charlie, Roman was not all right. He walked up to the door and put his ear against it. "Why? Why, Roman? How am I supposed to deal with this? I know what you are in there." He heard snuffling and could see a shadow move past the bottom of the door.

"Great. Now I got a wolf the size of God-fucking-zilla in my bathroom." He threw his coat and hat down in anger. "What do I do to change you back, Roman? Tell me. I don't get this." Charlie sat on the opposite side of the door, leaning his head against it. "I'm tired, babe. So tired. I don't know why you came to me. I don't know nuthin' about nuthin'. I'm just a simple cowboy from Utah."

The snuffling noises changed to something more human-like. Still, Charlie was not about to open the door. "All I want to do is take a piss and wash up. And I can't do that with a timber wolf in my bathroom." Charlie laughed sadly at the absurdity of his own comment. "Man, I am truly cracking myself up. And not in a good way, mind you."

"Charlie."

"Thank fuck." He stood and opened the door, peering in. Roman was on the floor curled up in a ball, looking like he was crying.

Charlie knelt down and brought Roman into his embrace, sitting with him. He sniffed his hair and through the shampoo scent he caught that musky smell he was beginning to understand. "Unreal. You smell like a wet dog. I kept trying to figure out why that smelled familiar."

"Great. What a turn on." Roman held Charlie close.

"You going to tell me what the hell all this is about?"

"I need to tell someone. I can't deal with this alone."

"If I get you out of here and on my bed, will I be fighting a wolf?"

Roman blinked, his green eyes so painfully lost, Charlie melted. He caressed Roman's black hair, petting it away from his forehead.

"I can't control it. I mean, I can a little, but not really."

"Well, ain't that a comfort." Charlie shook his head. "Come on then. I have to take my chances." He stood, taking Roman with him. "Let me wash up. Okay?"

"Yes." Roman made his way to the bed, slightly unsteady on his feet.

Charlie shut the door to urinate and get ready in private. He looked at himself in the mirror and noticed he was filthy from the night's work. He stripped off his clothing and stepped into the shower. Giving himself a quick wash, he filled the room with steam. Charlie then dried himself off and caught something strange in the mirror's reflection. He jumped back and looked behind him. Nothing was there. He wiped the mirror off and shouted out in fear before he could prevent it.

Roman rushed in. "What happened?"

Charlie wasn't sure he knew. He pointed to the mirror and couldn't believe what he had seen.

As if he understood, Roman deflated. "Great." He scuffed his heels to the bed.

Charlie gave the mirror a last look, shut the light and joined Roman on the bed. "I don't even want to ask you to start at the beginning. I know it's a long tale."

"You look as tired as I feel. I'm sorry about earlier. But that stupid Jack Russell is a pain in my ass."

"Yeah. That's Harley. But he don't want nothin' hurtin' our ponies. You have to give him some credit."

"I would never hurt an animal."

"Then it wasn't you that cut up that deer?"

"Hell no."

"Do you know who it was?"

Roman appeared grim. He tilted his head to the bathroom. "Her."

"Her." Charlie had no idea who Roman meant.

"You see that…that face in the mirror?"

"If you can call it a face." Charlie shivered.

"I think it's a shaman. You know what a shaman is?"

"I've heard things. This area is Ute land."

"Smart man." Roman tapped Charlie's head lightly. "I need you, my intelligent man."

"I have no connection to that tribe, Roman. I know very little."

"I'll tell you something else."

"I know you have a lot more to tell. I know." Charlie stifled a yawn.

"All right. I'll leave you with this to think about before I either turn into something stupid, or you fall asleep."

"What?"

"I'm an ATF agent and there's no gambling allowed in Utah. You think on that."

"Come here. You ain't no wolf yet." Charlie cupped the back of Roman's head and brought him to his lips. The more he touched the man, the more he liked it. "I am buyin' lube and rubbers before our next sexual bout. You got that?" Charlie chewed on Roman's jaw, nibbling his way to his neck. "I'm tryin' not to be nervous about you not usin' any last time."

"Sorry, babe. I'm clean. I promise." Roman sank into the mattress and moaned as Charlie began to play with him.

"Yeah. Any man can say that. And my ass is still smartin' from that humpin' you gave me." He ran his hand down Roman's chest to his abdomen.

"Sorry. I swear I didn't mean to be that rough. I just…"

Charlie kissed Roman's nipple. "Just…just turned into a wolf and mounted me like a bitch."

"Oh, Christ," Roman moaned and covered his eyes. "I'm sorry."

Charlie folded the blankets back and took a good look at Roman's body. "Maybe you have 'animal magnetism' or somethin', buddy, but I am very turned on by you. I mean, to the extreme."

"Ditto." Roman caressed Charlie's hair.

"You always prefer men?" Charlie ran his hand lightly over Roman's erection. It bobbed at the touch.

"Yes. Always."

Charlie caressed Roman's hot, soft balls, rolling them in his palm. "This is all new to me."

"I know." Roman smiled sweetly.

"I got turned on to man-love last October." Charlie pumped Roman's cock as he spoke, seeing his own thickening with excitement. "I had a flat tire on the highway and I was lucky enough for a pretty gay boy to stop and help."

"He took one look at you and figured it was *his* lucky day."

"I'm nothin' special." Charlie felt his cheeks blush.

"Wrong." Roman thrust his hips into Charlie's palm. "You are everything special. And the fact that you don't know it makes you even more amazing."

Charlie felt a lump in his throat. He cradled Roman's neck and kissed him again, this time, cupping his jaw, opening his mouth wider and using his tongue more aggressively.

Roman responded, embracing Charlie and grinding their cocks together.

When Charlie heard him growl, he tried to part from the kiss. Roman held on tight. His heart pumping from the attraction and intimidation, Charlie prayed Roman would stay human for this sexual bout. In an abrupt movement, Roman spun them over on the bed so he was on top.

Charlie blinked and held his breath.

Roman began to lick his way down Charlie's body. His whimpers turning more sensual, and unfortunately, more animalistic.

"Don't chew my dick off." Charlie was not kidding.

"Never." Roman nuzzled his face all over Charlie's body, as if exchanging scents with him. He began running long wet laps up Charlie's cock.

Charlie was not a religious man, but he said a silent prayer to keep Roman a man, begging for him not to turn canine on him.

Roman forced Charlie's legs apart strongly, rubbing his face between his thighs, over his balls and against his cock.

Chills and goose flesh coated Charlie's skin from the pleasure. Roman grabbed Charlie by the knees and pushed his legs upwards, exposing his ass. "Did I do that?" Roman asked.

"Do what?" Charlie had no idea what Roman was going to do to him with his legs straddled, but whatever it was it was going to be good. "Forget it. Keep goin'."

"I'm sorry I scratched you."

"Shut up, wolf-man and keep sucking my cock before you change into somethin' that can't."

"I can do better than that." Roman gave Charlie a wicked grin. He lowered himself on the bed and Charlie felt his rim being licked and tongue-fucked.

"*Oh*, babe. That's good. That's very good." Charlie grabbed his own cock and pulled on it. When Roman noticed, he nudged Charlie's hand aside and took over.

Roman's growling grew deeper and his mouth's actions much more aggressive.

Charlie had tingling rushes in every direction, originating at his groin. The fisting grew rougher, faster. "Sweet Lord!" Charlie arched his back as the need to come became urgent.

As if he knew how close Charlie was, Roman released Charlie's legs from their bent position and engulfed Charlie's cock down to the base.

Charlie thrust his hips hard into Roman's mouth, feeling his balls tighten and release their load. Charlie clenched his teeth before he was the one to howl like a wolf. He came so hard he felt he was levitating off the bed.

He opened his eyes to look, seeing Roman's expression of complete nirvana as he swallowed what Charlie had to give.

"Thank fuck you're still human." Charlie gasped to catch his breath.

Roman knelt upright, his cock thick and imposing. Charlie stared at it, then slowly made eye contact with Roman. His pupils were glowing, the way animal's eyes did in headlights.

Roman gripped his own cock in two hands, fisting it, and threw back his head, spurting cream all over Charlie as Charlie watched in awe. The deep guttural moan of Roman's began to change.

"Oh no." Charlie started retreating. "I see it coming. Sweet Jesus!"

Roman appeared to be battling the transition with every fiber of his being. Every sinewy muscle in Roman's body flexed and showed through his skin.

As a human, Roman was imposing. The first time Charlie had set eyes on him he could see how powerfully built Roman was. Big, strong and not a man he would ever want to battle with. But when Roman was a wolf, he was even more terrifying.

"Roman! Keep fightin' it!" Charlie had no idea how to help him. He knew if Roman turned, he'd have to get him the hell out of the cabin.

His fists clenched, his eyes closed, Roman's entire body went tense and hard. Then he snarled, showing his teeth.

"Oh crap!" Charlie stumbled off the bed. "Tell me what to do! Roman…I don't know how to stop this." Charlie used the wall to feel his way to the front door. He didn't want to take his eyes off Roman but had no choice. He opened the door a crack so Roman could get out and they wouldn't be trapped together while he was in that state.

Charlie crept back and peeked into the bedroom. A large black timber wolf was shaking off its coat like it had been in a river. "I cannot believe this. I seriously cannot believe this is happening."

Charlie kicked the bedroom door backwards opening it wider, and held his breath.

Of Wolves and Men

The wolf gave him one last saddened look. The pain in his eyes tore Charlie's heart and soul to shreds. "Door's open." Charlie didn't want to move.

Roman's ears perked up and he bolted outside.

Charlie closed the front door behind him, sliding down to sit on the floor and covering his face in his hands.

Chapter 7

The next morning, Charlie headed to the ranch house for his breakfast. He liked being the first one there to talk to Vernon about the day's schedule. The aroma of fresh brewed coffee, bacon, and sausage filled his senses the moment he opened the door. Vernon was kneeling by the fireplace adding logs. When he heard him he asked, "How you feeling, Charlie?"

"Good. Ready for a day of hard work."

At the sound of his voice, Suzie and Sherlane nearly knocked each other over trying to get out of the kitchen to greet him. Both had on aprons, and Sherlane held a spatula in her hand.

"Charlie!" Suzie rushed towards him. "We made a western omelet that's gonna knock your socks off."

"Come get it, Charlie." Sherlane craned her finger.

"You girls act like I'm the only eligible bachelor in the area." He laughed, taking off his hat while Suzie helped him with his coat. "I can do that, you silly girl."

She hugged the jacket in her arms and sniffed it.

"Oh, don't be doin' that. That thing's seen more dirt and sweat than you want to know. It needs a good dry cleanin'."

"I don't care." Suzie squeezed his coat like it was a teddy bear.

In the heat from the roaring fireplace, Charlie rolled up his sleeves and spotted Connie busy at the stove. "Mornin', Charlie. How're you feeling?"

"Very good, Connie. Thanks for askin'." He took the mug of coffee Sherlane handed him. "Thank ya, darlin'."

"Sit. I'll fix you up a nice helping."

Charlie sat in his usual spot at the long table. Next to the head, leaving it open for Vernon, who came into the kitchen and washed his hands. "Butch suggested we put out some leg traps up by the west fence."

Charlie felt as if he went ash white. "No. No, Vernon. Not a chance."

Vernon sat beside him and Suzie brought him a cup of coffee while Sherlane placed plates piled high with food in front of them.

Charlie said, "Thank ya, hun," and focused on Vernon. "First of all, them traps are indiscriminate killers. I hate them damn things. Poor critters gnaw off the own legs to get away. I'm surprised at you, Vernon."

"I'm at a loss, Charlie. What do you suggest?"

"One deer. That's it so far." Charlie ate a bite of the food, noticing both Suzie and Sherlane staring. He said, "Good, thanks."

They said, "You're welcome," in harmony.

Charlie cleared his throat and couldn't remember the girls being so enamored with him the last time they came home from college. "Anyway, boss, you let me handle things. Can you do that?"

"Butch says the fence is cut every day." Vernon ate as he spoke.

"And you think an animal is cutting barbed wire?" Charlie laughed in a cough. "Butch is an idiot."

"Am I?"

Both he and Vernon looked up as Butch, Goat, and JP entered the kitchen. The women got busy serving them coffee and breakfast.

Butch sat across from Charlie, setting his hat on his lap.

"No way am I lettin' you put out leg traps. They ain't ethical and there's a big controversy around them. You want this ranch caught up between the huntin' groups and the animal activists? Do we need that for our tourist business, boss?"

"They're legal. Just as long as we check 'em every two days." Butch began eating hungrily.

"Vernon, you have to be kiddin' me." Charlie felt sick to his stomach. "Will you let me deal with it?"

"One more butchered animal, Charlie," Vernon said holding up his finger. "And we put them out."

Charlie grew furious and pushed his plate of food away. "You've all lost your reason. Hear me out." He tried to calm down. "Doc McMurray tells you the damn deer was killed by a knife. Right? A human with a knife." He glared at Butch and then returned his stare to Vernon. "We got humans, not animals, cutting barbed wire. Are you all with me so far?" Charlie could see JP and Goat eating, trying to pretend they weren't part of the debate. "So you're intendin' on usin' those miserable leg-hold traps to kill animals that got nothin' to do with our human problem. You gettin' me, boss? No disrespect intended, sir, but I think Butch has got you all riled up over a human problem."

"Charlie just don't want to catch that wolf. Roman, he calls it." Butch smirked.

"What?" Goat laughed uneasily.

Charlie rubbed his forehead and ran his hand through his hair. "Butch, one more comment, and you an' me will take it outside."

Butch pushed out his chair violently in challenge.

Charlie stood up, wanting to kick his ass.

"Sit!" Vernon pointed his fork at them.

He and Butch exchanged glares, each knowing once they got outside the fight was on. But they both sat down.

Of Wolves and Men

Suzie topped up everyone's coffee cup. When she held the pot over Charlie's cup, he stopped her. "No more for me. And you can take this. I lost my appetite." He handed her the plate.

"You hardly touched it. Charlie, you have to eat." Suzie caressed Charlie's back.

Charlie again caught the jealousy in Butch's eyes. He addressed Vernon again. "Boss, I will not allow leg traps. We got no coyote problem. Nothin' is messin' with our ponies. And if you don't think your use of those things isn't going to mess with your trail ridin' business think again." Charlie shot Butch a look of fury. "He's thinkin' of himself, not you, not your ranch, your work. Have you thought about the long haul of usin' those things?" Charlie took a breath, trying to calm down. "I'll paint you a pretty picture, boss," he said sarcastically. "We got us a nice party of city folks all lookin' for a pretty leisurely ride in the mountains."

Vernon waved his hand for Suzie to not pour him more coffee, and focused on Charlie.

"Here we are, our nice little ridin' trail expedition," Charlie said, sneering, "Oh, lookie here." He pointed as if he were on the trail. "A poor baby deer with its leg in a steel trap. My, ain't that a nice memory to bring back to the folks back home?" He snarled at Butch, wishing he were a wolf at the moment and he could scare the crap out of him.

It didn't take Vernon more than a minute. "No traps, Butch."

"Thank you, Dad," Sherlane said, "They're inhumane and Charlie's right. Can you imagine some young child seeing that on our trail ride?" She shivered to show her point.

Butch wasn't the kind of man who liked to be wrong. He said, "Excuse me, ladies. Thank you for the meal, but I have work to do." He put his hat on and left.

Charlie exchanged glances with JP and Goat. None of them had a problem with Butch before so Charlie had no idea of what the two men were thinking.

"Can I have another helping?" Goat held up his plate to Suzie.

"Sure, Hal." The girls never called him 'Goat'.

Charlie leaned closer to Vernon. "I know it ain't my place, boss, to fire someone."

"You feel Butch is that bad of a worker I need to let him go?"

"Not a bad worker. No. But this last week, it's the bad attitude. He don't like me bein' the manager. I can see it in his eyes. He's angry now all the time." Charlie peeked behind him first before he said softly, "and very jealous of the girls' friendship with me."

"Yeah. That I know." Vernon chuckled.

"Here ya go, Hal." Suzie set another helping of food in front of him. "Can I get anyone anything else?"

The rest of the men shook their heads, saying, "No, thank you." She began clearing the table.

Connie walked up behind Charlie and caressed his back lightly. "You work with Butch, Charlie. We don't."

"I hate to lose him," JP said, "I got no complaints. He works hard, boss."

Charlie felt the same. Butch was a hard worker. "He's just becomin' a nuisance."

"Sit, Harley." Sherlane held a scrap of meat for the dog.

Charlie said, "Speakin' of a nuisance." He smiled. "You, dog!"

Vernon said, "He's just doin' his job. He thinks he's a Doberman Pinscher."

Charlie and the other boys laughed. "True." Charlie said, looking back as the dog begged for food.

~

Charlie headed out of the ranch house with the other two men. Just as he did, the truck filled with their wranglers arrived. Charlie stood by as they unloaded. Most of the men were sitting

Of Wolves and Men

in the open truck bed, while three were inside the cab. "Mornin' boys." Charlie greeted them.

They gave him a wave as they began their job of grooming the horses and mucking out the stalls.

Goat, JP, and Charlie walked to the stable to get their own duties underway. Charlie removed Spirit from his stall and led him to the open pasture while he shoveled horse droppings into a wheelbarrow.

He heard JP ask, "Where's Butch?"

Charlie poked his head out of Spirit's stall. He yelled Butch's name, looking in the direction of Scout's stall in the barn. "Ain't he here?"

"Nope. He's out somewhere and didn't clean Scout's stall either."

Charlie stewed as he continued his job. He didn't count on this unusual predicament. If Roman wasn't the wolf threatening the ranch, Charlie would be out trying catch him or scare him away. He wasn't sure he blamed Butch for his actions. They were well intended.

He tossed clean hay down on the floor of Spirit's stall, filled his water bucket and then wheeled the dirty hay to a truck and dumped it.

The other men were busy taking the horses out and brushing them, checking their shoes, and inspecting their condition before the tour groups arrived and they began a hike up into the hills.

Charlie called to Spirit and approached him. The horse stood still as he took a hold of his halter and brought him back to saddle up. "You and me got to take a ride, fella."

He tossed his saddle on Spirit's back and the bridle over his head. Once he was ready, Charlie swung his leg over the horse and sat tall. He waved to JP as he left. JP gave him a nod of his head, as if they both knew Charlie was going to see what Butch was up to.

He rode directly up the trail to the area with the cut fence line. Sure enough the barbwire was tampered with. Hopping down from Spirit, Charlie inspected the cut marks, and could easily tell they were from a wire clipper. He repaired the small opening quickly and heard Spirit snort. Charlie took a look at him and noticed his head was turned, looking back, his ears perked up.

"What is it?" Charlie stood, fixing his hat and tucking the tools back into the saddlebag. Hearing a noise, Charlie put his foot into the stirrup and mounted him, walking Spirit down an embankment to the reservoir. He spotted Scout standing idle, and Butch kneeling at the edge of the water, washing his hands. They were too far off to see well but Charlie thought it was odd. He began walking Spirit closer to have a conversation with Butch about him neglecting his duties back at the barn. The moment Butch heard them approach, he stood quickly, wiping his hands on his jeans, with an unreadable expression on his face. Charlie couldn't tell if it was anger or fear.

"Butch, what are you doin'?"

"I found another cut up deer."

Charlie's stomach knotted. "Where?"

"There." Butch pointed, climbing on Scout's back.

Suspicion began to invade Charlie's thoughts. But he was going to give Butch the benefit of the doubt. He followed him. As he drew near, he could see a deer carcass, steam rising out of its opened entrails.

Immediately Charlie knew. "Butch, please tell me you didn't do this to prove some demented point." He hopped off and could easily see the animal was just killed. It was still hot and bleeding, the cold air making it a mass of vapor trails waving in the breeze.

"Me?" Even his denial appeared cliché.

"Get down here." Charlie pointed to the ground.

Reluctantly Butch did.

Charlie grabbed his arm and inspected the cuff of his jacket. It had blood all over it. "Why? Why did you have to do this, Butch?"

Butch tugged his arm away. "I just wanted to prove to you we needed to do something."

"By faking this ritual thing?" Charlie pointed to the animal in disgust. "You do realize there're trail rides today." Charlie took out his cell phone. "I have to tell Vernon not to come near this area until we clean this up."

"Don't tell him it was me." Butch appeared threatening.

"You're jokin', right?" Charlie shook his head and stared at the deer as the line connected. "Vernon, look, don't bring them tourists up the west side."

"Why, Charlie? We got more trouble?"

"Yeah. We do." Charlie stared into Butch's eyes. "I'll tell ya later, boss."

"Okay. Thanks for the heads up."

Charlie shut off the phone and pocketed it. "*You're* goin' to tell him."

"He'll fire me."

"Yeah. He will." Charlie said, "Tie it up and let's take it out to the mountains. Ain't no reason she needs to go to waste. Let the coyotes gnaw on her." He knelt beside it. "Tell me you did not cut that animal's heart out." Seeing the sickness wash over Butch's expression, Charlie got his answer. "Ya know, I can see the buckshot in her. How would you explain that?"

"I was gonna say I shot at something near it."

"Butch…" Charlie stood and approached him. "What happened to you? You and I, we got on all right. I thought you were a bright boy in the interview me and Vernon had with you. I expected more from you."

"And I thought you would be a good friend, Charlie. But you're not the same either."

"How have I changed?" Charlie took his rope off his saddle and began to tie the hind legs of the dead deer together so they could drag it.

"I don't know. We used to go out and have a beer at the Other Side…now? Nothing. You won't even go out with the girls and me so I can get to know them better. Then you go and befriend some wolf and call him Roman."

Charlie stood with the end of the rope in his hand. "There ain't no Roman!" After he said it he glanced around to see if anything was watching them, particularly a crow. "And I don't want to go out with you and the girls." He tied the rope end around the horn on Butch's saddle.

"Why don't you? I know they're both keen on you. But once you pick one, I can date the other."

"Are you deaf? I am not datin' either of Vernon's girls." Charlie said, "Get in the saddle. Go."

"Don't tell Vernon, Charlie." Butch stood beside him.

"I have to. I can't keep somethin' like this from him." He tugged on the knot to make sure it was tight. "Now go on. Take her way out yonder where no one can find her but the scavengers."

Charlie waited but Butch didn't budge. "Why aren't you getting' on that horse, Butch?"

"Because I've a feelin' once I head that way," he pointed and said, "You'll go right to the ranch."

"I told you to go. It's up to you to clean up the mess you made. Bad enough this poor thing had to die like that. Not to mention that deer huntin' season ended last month."

"You're going to report me to fish and game too?"

"I've half a mind to!" Charlie was growing angry that Butch had already screwed up and now wanted complicity.

"I'll say you killed it! You and your wolf."

"Why do you keep goin' on that I own a wolf?" Charlie was fed up with this argument. "And I'm not the one with blood on my coat sleeves. You are."

"Charlie, don't. I need this job." Butch grabbed Charlie's lapels.

"Then listen when I tell you to do somethin' and stop actin' like a fool." Charlie brushed Butch's hands off his jacket.

"I swear, Charlie, don't tell no one about this! It's just you and me up here, and no one has to know."

Throwing up his hands in frustration, Charlie replied, "I can't do that. You think I want to be involved with your messy deeds? I have enough to worry about." He pushed Butch to the horse. "Now take this carcass up the mountain."

"Don't you push me." Butch spun around and glared at him.

"Fine! You know what?" Charlie took his mobile phone out of his pocket. "I was goin' to try and help you after you explained it to Vernon, but now? I'm goin' to have Vernon ride up here to see this for himself."

Butch whacked the phone out of Charlie's hand and it scattered to the frozen ground, skidding off under the brush.

"You son of a bitch." Charlie puffed up. "You think this is helpin' you?"

Butch reached for something on his belt. Charlie knew the man had to have his knife with him to have done the damage he did to the doe. He could see both of their shotguns hanging from Spirit and Scout's saddles. Charlie grabbed Butch's right wrist and held tight. Butch's fingers were gripped around a five-inch fixed-blade knife.

"Don't be stupid!" Charlie tried to get Butch to drop the knife, twisting his arm. "You goin' to kill me? You think that'll get you out of, or *into,* more hot water?"

"Don't matter now!" Butch began struggling with Charlie. "You're going to make me lose my work, report me to fish and game... I'm going to lose everything as it is."

Charlie held the knife hand over Butch's head and grabbed him around the neck with his free hand, trying to trip him backwards. "You'll lose even more in the state lock-up, you bonehead!"

Butch fell backwards, nearly into Scout. The horse shifted away but didn't go far with the deer carcass attached to its saddle.

Charlie fell with him, not relenting his grip on the wrist holding the knife. "Let it go, you stupid boy!" He had Butch pinned under him, slamming his hand over and over again against the rocks and hard soil to loosen his hold.

Butch opened his fingers and the knife dropped out of his hand. He lay panting under Charlie, his eyes welling up. "Charlie, please."

"You don't leave me a whole lotta' choices, Butch." Charlie made a move to stand, reaching for the knife.

Before Charlie did, Butch gripped him by both shoulders, making Charlie search his eyes. "I need this job." Butch bit his bottom lip. "I'm so jealous of you…"

"Why? I don't get that."

"You got all the girls after you… Vernon likes you best." Butch seemed embarrassed by a tear that ran down his face. He wiped it roughly.

Charlie rolled to his side so he and Butch's crotches weren't pressed together. "I don't want to date Vernon's daughters, for the hundredth time. And I've worked longest here, so me and Vernon are close. That's it."

"No…no…"

Charlie stood holding the knife at this side. "I'm not sure what's goin' on in your head, Butch." He tucked the knife into the saddlebag on Spirit's back and picked up his phone where it lay under some brush. He heard a loud squawk and spun around.

The crow was perched close by on a low branch, eying him.

Butch stood slowly, straightening his jacket and hat. "It ain't that, Charlie. You know why."

Charlie tried to think. "No. I don't know why." He mounted Spirit. "Come on. I'll walk with you to get rid of the deer." He watched Butch swing his leg over the saddle, looking defeated and not like the eager young man he'd been only a week ago.

Scout began dragging the dead doe as Charlie walked Spirit beside them. "I reckon we should bring her way deep off the trail. Vernon's got bookings all week, ya know."

"Yeah. I know."

"Nineteen," Charlie said, giving Butch a glance from under the brim of his hat. "By now, I would have thought you'd be more sensible."

"I am. I just do stupid things."

Charlie laughed at the accurate appraisal. The crow flapped close to where they were. He could feel the gust from its large wingspan. With the crow keeping them company, they walked silently to the thick line of evergreens inside the federal land area.

"That bird is just dying for a free meal." Butch tilted his head to the carcass.

Charlie looked over his shoulder and found it hitching a ride on the dead deer as it was dragged. "I suppose it's got to eat somethin'." Charlie addressed the bird, "Wouldn't you rather have pork chops and hash?"

The bird tilted its head but kept its balance as the horse's gait jerked the rope.

"How about here?" Charlie stopped Spirit and hopped off.

When Butch did the same, he waved at the bird to scare it off. "Shoo."

The crow didn't move.

"That can't be the same bird from the other day, can it?" Butch untied the rope from his saddle. "If it is, he don't scare easy."

"No. I know he don't." Charlie gave the bird a scolding glance. He crouched down and untied the legs of the deer releasing the end of the rope so Butch could coil it up.

"Thanks, Charlie."

"You won't thank me when I make you talk to Vernon."

"I know."

"And you still need to muck Scout's stall. No one's goin' to do it for you."

Butch secured the rope to Scout's saddle and stared at the bird. "Why isn't he eating it?"

"Maybe he doesn't like to be watched." Charlie worried that Roman would suddenly change into something else, like a naked man or a wolf. Either way, he didn't need Butch here to see it.

"Come on. Let's go." Charlie mounted Spirit and turned her one hundred and eighty degrees.

The bird began flapping its wings wildly and shaking its head.

"Uh oh." Charlie had a bad feeling. "Butch, get a move on."

"Why?"

"'Cause it's time to go." Charlie raised his voice, "Sometimes you have to do things without askin' why."

Butch leapt onto Scout.

"Now go!"

"You coming?"

"In a minute." Charlie could see Butch's curiosity. "Did I just tell you to get a move on? Come on, Butch. You want me to defend you to Vernon? After this?" He pointed to the deer. "After comin' at me with a knife?"

"I get it!" Butch used his boot heels to urge Scout to walk.

Charlie followed only far enough to watch as Butch continued down the trail. The minute Butch vanished from sight, Charlie hurried back to the crow.

Sure enough, Roman was rolling on the grass beside the deer, appearing to be in pain.

Charlie leapt off Spirit and hurried to Roman's side. He held him in his lap, rocking him. "All right..."

"I can't keep doing this, Charlie." Roman's teeth were clenched as if the constant transitions were agonizing. "Use that fucking knife on me."

"No way." Charlie opened his jacket and embraced Roman, wrapping the warm sheepskin around his nakedness. "All right, babe...I'm here." Charlie rested his head on Roman's shoulder and closed his eyes. "How do I help you? Hm? How?"

"Find the shaman who cursed me into this hell."

"How do I find him?"

"Her. Not a him."

Spirit once again appeared uneasy at Roman's presence and his ears flapped back a few times as if he couldn't decide what to do. Charlie said to him, "Don't you go nowhere, you damn horse."

"He smells the wolf on me."

"I figured that out. Can you stand? Do you need to come back to the cabin and eat? I mean, I assume you weren't really goin' to peck at the deer."

"That idiot shot it, then cut out its heart! And you played nice?"

"You let me deal with Butch." Charlie tried to get Roman to his feet.

"He's got a hard-on for you." Roman's legs trembled as he managed to stand.

"Nope. He's got two hard-ons, one for each Norman sister."

"You can't read his mind."

"And I don't want to." Charlie stood beside Spirit as the whites of his eyes began to show as Roman drew closer. "How am I going to sneak you in? There's a barn load of wranglers down there, not to mention JP, Goat, Vernon..."

"I'm all right. You go."

"I am not leavin' you like this."

Roman cupped Charlie's jaw and kissed him. Charlie kept the rein in his fist but still managed to embrace Roman. With his free hand, he ran his fingers up and down Roman's muscular build. As the kissing increased in intensity, Charlie felt Roman rub his stiff length over his jeans.

"I got to get you to stay a man. I want you, Roman. Real bad." Charlie reached between them, feeling Roman's cock as it thickened and pointed upright. While he stroked Roman's cock, Charlie closed his eyes and enjoyed the hungry kisses running up and down his neck, his earlobe, and his jaw.

"Tie that horse up so I can make love to you."

Charlie blinked and looked at Spirit who wasn't at all happy with Roman's close proximity to him. He released his embrace and tied the rein to the nearest tree. He peered back at the deer. "Can we not screw right on top of that thing?"

"You wanna screw me?" Roman wrapped his arms around Charlie's waist and picked him up off the ground.

"Yeah. And I have to get into town and find enough courage to buy lubrication. Condoms I can handle. But lube? Don't that say queer all over it?"

"Yeah." Roman lowered them both to the ground, nibbling Charlie's cheek and neck as he unbuttoned his shirt. "Tell me how queer you are, handsome."

Charlie chuckled. "Looks like I'm the new gay boy in town." He watched Roman open his clothing, spreading it wide.

At Roman's touch, Charlie relaxed under him, beginning to pant and sweat as Roman worked his way downwards. When his cock was fully engulfed in Roman's mouth, Charlie moaned and closed his eyes. *How do I keep you? Hm? How?*

"It isn't going to be in a kennel or a birdcage."

"Stop readin' my mind. Be quiet and finish what you started." Charlie raised his hips. Roman went back to sucking. Charlie closed his eyes and focused on the pleasure only. He let go of the chaos for now. They'd figure it out. Somehow.

As the sensation began to rise, Charlie gripped Roman's head through his thick black hair. He fucked Roman's mouth, not having intended to be rough, but it felt so good. Roman whimpered in delight, quickening his pace and suction until Charlie was over the edge. "I'm there, babe..." Charlie threw back his head and climaxed, trying to silence the grunts of pure pleasure.

He kept his fingers locked in Roman's head of hair as Roman milked him, sucking the last drops. When he sat up, Roman pumped his own cock, giving Charlie a wicked smirk.

Still recuperating from a mind-blowing blowjob, Charlie nudged Roman to his back and knelt over him, taking his turn. He closed his eyes and inhaled, trying to smell Roman's masculine scent over any animal aromas. He tasted incredible, and the way Roman's balls tightened in his fingers drove Charlie wild.

Roman began thrusting and moaning as he rose to a climax. Charlie didn't look. Last thing he wanted to see was that he was giving a timber wolf head. But the touch of Roman was still human flesh.

"Charlie! Holy fuck..." Roman raised his hips high and deepened his penetration of Charlie's mouth.

Charlie gripped the base and held it firm as it pulsated and shot a load into his mouth. He moaned as well, swallowing it down, enjoying this man on man loving more each time.

The sound of Roman's gasping breaths echoed in Charlie's ears.

Roman nudged Charlie off. "Oh, God...no... Charlie, go!"

Charlie jumped to his feet and began fixing his clothing staring at Roman as he once again fought off the change.

Spirit went nuts, stomping and rearing, threatening to tear off the tree limb and bolt.

"I said go!" Roman rolled to his front and began shaking while on his hands and knees.

"I can't stand seein' you go through this." Charlie picked up his hat from the ground, dying inside.

The growl coming from Roman was terrifying. Charlie grabbed Spirit who was on his hind legs trying to get away.

One last word from Roman, "Go!" and Charlie hopped on Spirit and rode off, wiping his eyes with the backs of his hands he was so upset. He caught something from the corner of his eye, but when he turned to look nothing was there. He galloped back to the ranch, trying to get his emotions under control.

Chapter 8

Charlie dusted off his hat and jeans after he had put Spirit into the open paddock. He looked for Scout.

"JP," Charlie called to the man putting hay out into the fields for the horses to graze.

"Yeah?"

"Didn't Butch come back?"

"Not yet."

A ball of ice filled Charlie's belly. He was about to head into the ranch house when JP said, "There's the lazy bastard now."

Butch was walking Scout down the path Charlie had just returned from. He caught a gleam in Butch's eye even from under the brim of his hat.

Charlie spun on his heels and stormed towards the ranch house to speak to Vernon. This had to be the last straw. He had no doubt Butch had seen he and Roman together. No doubt at all.

"Charlie!" Suzie greeted him with enthusiasm. "We were just going to call you boys down for lunch."

"Where's your dad, Suzie?"

"In his study. Is everything okay?"

"Yeah. You go call the boys for lunch, and tell the wranglers they can break and go eat."

"Sure thing, Charlie." Suzie gave him a look of concern as she left the house.

Charlie walked down a hallway, took off his hat, and stood by the door. "Vernon?"

"Come in, Charlie." Vernon put the paperwork he was reading down on his desk and asked, "So? We got another mutilated animal up at the west fence?"

Closing the door, Charlie sat down on the chair in front of the desk and put his hat on his lap. "Butch killed it, makin' it look like another ritual slaughter."

Vernon's eyes widened and he opened his mouth but said nothing.

"When I first got up that end, he was washin' his hands in the reservoir. Didn't matter. He had blood all over his coat sleeves."

"Charlie, no. Why would the boy do that?"

"He's tryin' to undermine me, Vernon." Charlie shook off his jacket, leaving it behind him on the chair. "My guess is if I hadn't have caught him literally red-handed, he would have justified his leg-trap idea."

"So you're telling me Butch just killed a deer off season, and…"

"And cut its fuckin' heart out."

Vernon rubbed his face as he digested the information.

"Vernon!" Butch knocked loudly on the door. "Vernon, don't listen to him!"

"Get in here, Butch." Vernon stood, breathing fire.

Butch entered the room, panting loudly, as if he sprinted to the house to try and stop this conversation. "He's a liar!"

"Sit down." Vernon pointed to another chair near the wall.

"Charlie?" Butch nudged him roughly. "You ever suck a man's cock?"

Charlie stiffened up but didn't make eye contact. *Shit. Goddamn-mother-fucking shit!*

"Take a look at this, Vernon." Butch handed Vernon his mobile phone. "I took them photos just now. Just now!"

Vernon had no choice but to look at the phone as it was shoved under his nose.

Charlie felt like a cornered cat. "What I do in my private life ain't like what you did up there to that deer!"

"Private?" Butch pushed a button on the phone as if changing the screen and held it in front of Vernon to look. "I don't think doing what you did with that naked man on ranch property was very private. What if our trail riding tour saw that? Huh? What if all them little kids we have riding up here, saw that!" Butch huffed, nodding his head like he had it all figured out.

"Get out." Vernon waved Butch to the door.

"But, boss!"

"I said, get out. I'll deal with you later." Vernon sat back down in his chair.

As he left, Butch said, "An' you call me the liar, the one with the problem."

Charlie shifted uncomfortably, sweat beginning to coat his skin. He didn't say a word. He was guilty.

"Charlie…"

"I'm sorry, Vernon. I was dead wrong."

"I…I always thought you were a real man's man."

"I'm not comfortable talking about this, boss."

"The girls will be so disappointed. As am I."

"Right. So now the fact that Butch killed an' eviscerated a deer off season, tried to stab me with his knife when I confronted him—"

"Let me have a moment." Vernon waved him off. "I need a minute."

Charlie grabbed his hat and coat and left the office, closing the door. When he walked into the living room area, everyone stopped talking. Butch had his camera-phone in his hand.

"More show and tell, Butch?" Charlie put his coat on.

"Charlie," Sherlane said, "Don't leave. Come eat lunch."

Charlie made eye contact with JP and Goat. They didn't look angry, just nervous, as if he was a threat to their manhood. Without another word, Charlie left the ranch house.

He sat behind the wheel of his pickup truck and drove out of the long drive to the main street. He was so upset with Butch's actions, the fact that he had been outted without time to even think about his own sexuality, and the turnaround of what had been Butch's demise becoming his own.

After a half hour of driving, Charlie pulled into the lot of the Other Side Tavern. He shut off the truck engine and climbed out, stuffing his keys into his pocket as he opened the entrance door.

It was dim and smelled like stale alcohol. Men were playing pool, darts, or watching sports on TV.

Charlie approached the bar. When he was given attention he said, "I'd like a beer, please."

"Certainly. Anything to eat from the kitchen?"

"I'll have a think on that." Charlie removed his wallet from his pocket and tossed money on the counter. He took the cold glass and sat down at a table in the corner. Once settled, his hat on the chair beside him, his coat tossed over the back of the seat, Charlie sipped it, staring off into space.

Chapter 9

A group of ATF special agents gathered at headquarters for a briefing.

Wearing a black t-shirt and black cargo pants, Roman sat on top of a desk while his supervisor, Nick Hoffman, spoke.

"Our role is one of back up and information gathering."

Roman was only identifiable as an agent by his badge and gun, hanging from his belt at the moment. Once the men figured out their involvement in this new assignment, they'd know how to dress.

"There's a rogue group running guns, booze, and illegal tobacco over in Utah, just southeast of Salt Lake City. The local police think it's the Indian Reservation occupants. Casinos are illegal in Utah, so word is they set up some underground gambling houses and are using heavy artillery to defend it."

Roman glanced at the squad of men he worked with. They were well-trained, he trusted them, and liked them. He was also out and none of them gave a shit about his sexual preference, which increased his respect for them even more.

"So our job, and the Feds' job, is to act as intel for the state and local sheriff's office. The Feds are sending in some agents as well who will assist us." Nick pointed to Roman. "Burk, you and Dean do some background work on the tribal nations in that area."

Roman nodded. Philip Dean caught his eye, acknowledging it as well.

"We'll regroup at the UHP in Salt Lake City once we do a little ground work." He checked his watch. "Any questions?"

As several men spoke to the lead agent, Roman said to Phil, "Looks like we got the easy part for a change."

"For now." Phil glanced at the men around them. "Wait until we find the cache of weapons. Then the real fun begins."

An hour later, he and Phil had all their gear loaded up in the trunk of their SUV; laptop computers, SWAT uniforms, and AK assault rifles. They hit Interstate 80 and drove from Reno to Salt Lake City in a caravan of black cars and SUVs. Roman was excited. New work in a different state, backing up local sheriff's departments, that's what he lived for.

He and Phil checked into a hotel room near the Utah Highway Patrol headquarters. An hour later, they were sitting at their computers tapping into the history of the Ute and Shoshoni tribes, checking names against their computer data bases.

"Not one with a criminal record." Phil scratched his head and yawned. "Other than traffic violations."

"You think they got it wrong? What if it's not the tribe setting up the illegal gaming. I've known biker groups to do more damage to the local area than Native Americans."

"I suppose that's what we're here to figure out." Phil tapped more keys on the laptop.

While Phil was at the desk in the hotel room, Roman sat propped up against the headboard of one of the double beds, his computer on his thighs. "The guys giving you any shit for rooming with me?"

"Nope. Not a bit. They know you better than that. And I hope they know I'm straight and can't be turned even by a guy like you, Burk."

Roman smiled as he browsed through web information for any indication of biker groups infiltrating the area. "I don't have time for a relationship anyway. In this job, all we do is travel."

"I hear ya. I think most of the guys who started this work with a wife have gotten divorced."

"True."

Roman's cell phone rang. He flipped it out of his pocket and said his name, "Burk…" knowing it was his lead supervisor.

"Got a tip from the sheriff's office over in a town called Heber that something's going on right now. Gear up and meet at UHP."

"Right." Roman began closing down his computer. "Gear up. They found something."

"Now we're talking." Phil stood up and hoisted his duffle bag onto the foot of his bed. "Show time."

A small army consisting of FBI, ATF, Utah Highway Patrol, and local Heber sheriff's officers stood in a meeting place in a parking lot a quarter mile from their target location.

Roman's group of officers was also SWAT trained and part of the Violent Criminal Enterprise apprehension team. They dealt with the worst offenders, explosive devices, and heavy weapons violations.

His lead ATF agent and the lead FBI agent were running the operation. Roman's heart was already pounding with adrenaline; his helmet under his arm, his AK hanging from his shoulder, armored up like a marine about to fight Afghan terrorists. Roman loved this part of his job best. Intel was one thing, but front line battle? Nothing better.

They had already studied the map and the floor plan of the building they were entering, had a rough idea of the types of weapons, including ingredients used to manufacture bombs, and each unit was assigned an entry point or post.

"Any questions?" Nick asked the men.

No one said a thing.

"Let's go!"

Roman put his helmet on and climbed into the back of an armored personnel carrier. As the truck moved, no one spoke, each mentally preparing for the danger ahead.

Though all of the men had been tactically trained with basically the same guidelines, working with local sheriff's departments, or Highway Patrol, wasn't easy. The FBI units did well with theirs. It was all the same strategy. But the smaller departments needed to step back and let the big boys take over.

He felt the vehicle halt, and they immediately exited the back of the truck. In the darkness, Roman and his men followed the lead agents who used hand signals.

His face shield down, his AK in his hands, Roman and his crew began to surround a huge warehouse building which looked from the outside as abandoned and dilapidated.

His group of six men made their way quietly to a steel back door. Nick held up his hand and they stopped moving as a unit.

All Roman could hear besides his own pounding heart and heavy breathing was the excited respiration of the men behind him. He knew the adrenaline dump pre-entry, and the high level of testosterone that was flowing in each man's veins. He could smell it.

"Police! Search warrant!" was yelled from the front.

A loud smash of the battering ram hitting the door was next.

Nick made a signal. The biggest man in their unit rammed the back door with a metal battering ram. It only took him one powerful hit to punch it open.

They flooded the building and raised their flashlights up with their AK rifles and fanned out. All the while Roman could hear the agents identifying themselves in loud voices, "FBI! Search warrant!" "ATF agents! Come out with your hands up!" as they went room to room.

From the back door, his group encountered nothing. No fleeing hoards of crooks or shots fired. Not a sound of commotion, but it was a very large building, and they needed to go floor by floor.

The front entry team and rear unit met up. "Nothing yet. Go check each room," Nick said. "My men, take the second and third floor. Feds, go up to the top and work down."

Roman and the rest of the team began their ascent up an exposed stairway that was more like a fire escape ladder than an interior staircase in a factory building. It shook with the combined weight of big, muscular men and heavy SWAT gear.

Roman and Phil peeled off from the group to search their area. They signaled the rest to move on. He and Phil had done the routine so often they knew each other's movements before they met gazes or exchanged signals.

One by one, Roman and Phil cleared the massive maze of rooms. The only thing inside each graffiti-tagged space was garbage, broken office furniture, newspapers, used condoms, hypodermic needles, and dead rats. And it stunk of urine and age. The plasterboard walls peeled from moisture, and the floor was rotted.

Not a sign of current inhabitation or any clandestine activity met Roman's eyes. But they had a long way to go before they were done.

They approached the end of the hall; an open door was at each side. Roman gave a sign to Phil he'd take the left, and Phil should move right.

Roman held his rifle upright and entered the room, pointing his flashlight around the perimeter. A strong smell hit him. But it didn't seem toxic, more herbal. But it overpowered him with its potency, not to mention the surprise of smelling anything other than decay, mold, piss, and dust.

On the walls were different symbols. These were not gang signs or swear words like in all the other rooms. A red inverted pentagram was mostly whitewashed over and other signs were covering it, as if to negate its terrible message. Roman was about to shout, "Clear!" to Phil when, in the pitch blackness, he caught something shadowy moving out of the corner of his eye. He spun around and pointed his AK and flashlight. Nothing was there.

"Clear, Roman." Phil poked his head into the room, telling Roman he had found nothing in his own search.

"Okay." Roman lowered the gun and was about to join Phil to regroup and see if anyone had found anything, but something held him back.

A heavy red mist blinded him temporarily, blocking his path to the hall. Roman waved his gloved hand in front of himself to try and see through it. It made him cough and his flashlight didn't seem to permeate it.

Dizziness hit him next. He reached out to the wall, trying to prevent falling. "Phil." He coughed harder, unable to shout loudly because this toxic air was in his throat. *Once Phil realizes I'm not behind him, he'll come back. No one is left behind on any mission. Ever.*

The darkness seemed to deepen and his flashlight fell from his gloved hand, shutting off as it hit the floor. Roman dropped to his padded knees, feeling sicker by the minute, wondering what he had stumbled into. He hoped no one else was suffering the same fate. A terrible fear that they'd been set up, and this was a trap to kill them, rushed over Roman.

"Roman?" Phil called out.

He tried to answer, "In here", but choked and coughed on his words. He fell to his back, the gun still clutched in his hand, but it felt as if someone were tugging at it to get it away from him.

In the blackest of shadows, a female form, but not a normal woman, was standing over him. Her face was painted bright red with white and blue markings under her eyes. A crest of black feathers topped the upper half of a wolf's skull, with its fur skin draped on her head. She held something in each hand and Roman heard chanting.

Bile rose in his throat. He turned his head to the side in case he threw up.

"Roman!"

Phil's voice seemed frantic. Roman couldn't figure out what was taking him so long. Surely Phil was only down the hall and knew where he had last seen him.

A black bird was hanging over his chest. The woman had it dangling by its feet in her hands. She cut its neck and blood spattered Roman's face shield and body armor. The chanting was making his ears ring.

"Roman, you fucker! Where the hell are you?"

Roman used all his willpower to move, to yell, to shake this haze, but all he could do was lay prone while something wicked began to possess him.

"I can't find Roman!" Phil's voice was panic stricken. "He was just in this room! Roman! Where the hell are you?"

Roman was beyond confused. An army of men were looking for him, but he was still in the same place. Wasn't he?

He rocked side to side on his back, like a tortoise that can't right itself. His gun dropped from his hand and he heard it clatter with a loud echo. The red painted woman knelt between Roman's bent knees. When he felt pressure against his groin area, he tried to jerk away. *Phil!* he was shouting in his brain and had no idea if sound was coming out.

"He must have moved down the hall to the stairs. Spread out. No one leaves without him."

Hearing a language he did not understand, being assaulted by a phantom woman who scared the hell out of him, not to mention his own helplessness, was beginning to make Roman crazy. In his head he shouted, *Leave me alone!,* rocking his body side to side to try and avoid the contact she was making with his genitals.

He felt naked. Icy cold. How that could be possible with the amount of heavy armor and clothing he was wearing was beyond him. Against his will she was rolling his testicles in her palm, fingering his limp length.

I'm dreaming. I have to be. What the fuck is going on?

He made the effort of looking down at his own body in the pitch darkness, touching himself. All his ATF clothing and weaponry were gone. Suddenly he had the illusion he was lying on the ground under a canopy of tall trees and firelight surrounded him. In the flickering flames, shadows passed. The chanting grew deeper, vibrating his ribcage, but stronger, as if fifty humans were surrounding him, all saying the same thing. As the silhouettes danced, they either touched him where he did not want to be touched, spattered animal blood on him from slit necks of birds, or coated him in dripping blood from what looked to be beating hearts.

He no longer heard the men's voices he worked with, nor their heavy tread on the stairs or hall. Forcing his eyes to open, he saw a full moon in a black sky.

Why me? Why me? Roman tried to keep his head, but it wasn't easy. *Am I high on toxic fumes? What did I walk into?*

As his entire body was painted blood-red by dozens of hands, Roman closed his eyes and imagined his sacrifice would be next. He just couldn't understand how he had gone from an armed group of men in a vacant building, to naked and helpless as a newborn under the black velvet sky. He imagined he never would figure it out, because he'd be dead by morning.

~

Roman awoke.

The scent of pine was extreme in his nose. He rubbed his eyes and was scratched by a claw on the end of his limb. He blinked. His arm was an animal's arm with a large paw. Roman tried to stand but ended up on all fours. He sat and attempted to see what he was. The terror of the sight of a black furry tail and huge paws instead of feet made him shriek. But he howled and made squeaking noises when he tried to talk. He spun around in a circle, trying to break free of himself, of the sensations. But all he did was get dizzy. He stopped moving and panted, feeling a long tongue and sharp canines.

This has to be a dream. I'm in the hotel. Aren't I? And Phil is in the next bed?

Roman raced through the woods, looking for something familiar. The smells were overwhelming him. Animal urine, pungent musky scents of deer or elk. And each tree gave off a unique aroma that was driving him insane. It was overwhelming him. His ears were picking up sounds from every direction. He halted again, looking down at his own paws. *What the fuck? Am I a dog? What did they do to me?*

He smelled water; the aroma of algae or wet plants. He followed it to an enormous reservoir. Walking gingerly into the shallows, Roman tried to see his reflection. In the blurry moving lake all he could make out was a long snout and big furry ears. He screamed and a yelp came out as he jolted backwards. *No. No way.*

Suddenly pain seized him. He fell over instantly and began shaking. The agony was so intense, he was certain he would pass out from it. He extended his arms and legs, seeing stiff furry paws with black hair and nails. He moaned and rolled side to side on his back, wishing he could cry, but he never was able to.

As he watched, his own hands began to appear, human hands. *Thank God! It's just a stupid dream! Wake up, Roman, wake up!*

He rested on his elbows, seeing that his chest and thighs, and thankfully, his dick were all in one piece. He was filthy and appeared to be coated in dried blood or something that had once been sticky and was now caked on. Unsteadily he got to his feet and returned to the water. He dove in and scrubbed at the dirt and reddish marks, washing them off, shivering in the icy water but feeling more himself and refreshed. He rinsed the water through his hair and then climbed out of the lake, beginning to get cold. He rubbed his arms to warm them, and started looking for help.

Even with the sun high in the sky, the air was icy cold. He shivered and couldn't seem to find his way out of the woods. He knew on a map where his team was, he just had no idea which direction he should go to find a phone or house.

A shiver ran up his spine and he stumbled and fell. Another episode of pain was starting up again. "No! No way! You have to be kidding me!" Roman clenched his fists. "I am not turning into a dog! No!" He stared at his hands and his fingers became long black feathers. "That's it. I'm on drugs. Someone captured me and is injecting LSD into my veins. Is that it?" He looked around the tall canopy of trees. "Am I a hostage being tortured?" he screamed at lung capacity before his voice turned into a squawk.

He hopped up and down flapping his arms which were now wings. *I've lost my mind. I'm in some nightmare I can't wake up from! What was in that abandoned building? What the hell happened to us? Us? Or just me?*

He flapped frantically, becoming airborne, panicking and landing again. He looked at his wingspan and spread out his arms. *Fine. I'm a fucking bird. Fly somewhere.*

He began flapping once more and did lift up. Instead of being terrified, he tried to steer. It was a skill he did not find easy. He hit a branch and tumbled down to the hard ground. Getting back to his little black feet, with long sharp talons, he flapped again, as vigorously as he could and got better and better with each attempt. *My luck I'll be a mile overhead and change into a man, plummeting back to earth. Yeah, go on, Roman, keep dreaming. You love flying dreams.*

With another few tries, Roman was able to figure out the skills he needed to turn, slow down, and speed up. It was easier recon from the air than the forest. He looked over the deserted roadways until he noticed a hotel with a load of sedans and SUVs in the lot. Men were there, grouped together.

My guys! I found you!

He practically hit the ground beak first beside them and waddled closer.

"Holy crap!" one of the men said, stepping aside. "That's one big black bird. What's wrong with it?"

No! No, guys! It's me! Roman! He flapped to help him move faster and made his way to Phil.

"What am I supposed to tell his family?" Phil asked Nick.

"I have no idea. Say he's gone MIA temporarily. Until I find a sign of foul play or his dead body, I'm not going to tell his family he's dead."

Dead? Phil! It's me! Roman poked his beak into Phil's boot.

"What the fuck?" Phil kicked at Roman. "Stupid thing. Christ, they grow big crows out here in Utah."

No. Come on, guys! Why would a bird come here and peck at you! It's me!

"Want me to shoot it?" one of the men asked. "It's probably got something wrong with it."

Roman spotted him pulling his gun out of his holster. He took off to the roof top in fear and the man put his gun away.

"So?" Phil said, "That's it? He's MIA on a job and…?"

"What the hell do you want me to say? We searched that building for forty-eight hours, had over a hundred officers, evidence techs, dogs sniffing for a track… You tell me where he went."

"That room. That last room." Phil thumbed over his shoulder as if the vacant building were behind them. "Something about the graffiti on the walls, the ritual burnings, the signs of sacrifice…that's the last place I saw him."

"And? So now he's been sacrificed? Is that what you want me to tell his family, Dean?"

"No. I mean, I don't know. But I do know that has to have something to do with it."

Roman glided back to the parking lot, feeling like an idiot because he knew he was walking like a duck. He stood in front of Phil again and tried to catch his attention. *Hello? Guys? I'm right here.*

"It's back. Shoot it. Something is very weird about that thing. Birds never come this close to humans."

Roman spun around and squawked loudly. A blast of a nine millimeter bullet just missed him. He took off for the high power lines and stopped, trying to balance on it.

"Leave it alone." Phil shook his head. "Don't we have enough to worry about?"

Roman watched as Phil placed his bag of equipment into the SUV. *How am I going to let them know?* Roman flapped his wings. *I want to be a man again. I want to be a man again.* He waited. He wasn't changing. *Now! I need to be me to show them I'm alive!*

The car doors slammed loudly, scaring him. He watched as one by one the ATF vehicles left the lot, back to Reno most likely. Did they even find what they came to Utah for? Had they given up? *Are you guys giving up on me?*

He flew alongside Phil's car as he drove, trying to get his attention. Phil appeared either furious or freaked out to see a bird so close to his driver's window.

Open the door! It's me, Phil! Me, Roman!

Phil powered the window down and took a swipe at him. "Get away, you crazy bird!"

Seeing Phil nearly crossing the double yellow line and hitting someone head on, Roman landed on a fence post and watched the caravan of cars leave.

He blinked his bird eyes and wondered if he sighed what it would sound like in bird talk.

This ain't a goddamn dream. I am in deep trouble.

Of Wolves and Men

Two days of flip-flopping from man to wolf to bird to man to wolf, Roman was exhausted and losing hope. The easiest way to find food was in his bird stage, picking at the leftovers from the fast food chains. Their litter was the most common and Roman managed to find enough burgers and fries to keep him full.

Walking aimlessly one afternoon, wolf-Roman heard men's voices. He sat on his hind legs and observed men on horseback rounding up a herd of horses. Sniffing the air and smelling their sweat, Roman missed making love, kissing a man.

When he began to daydream about the sex he'd previously had with some very hot men, his cock grew hard and he began to turn human. Lying naked on someone's horse ranch with a big erection wasn't going to get him help, it was going to get him killed or beaten.

Roman crawled to the shadows of underbrush and tried to hide.

A man on horseback drew closer. "Get them ponies in for the night."

"Okay, Charlie!"

Charlie. Roman took a good look at the handsome cowboy. He looked like a gay man's fantasy with his big brawny build and blue eyes.

Suddenly Roman heard the man's thoughts. He shut up his own and listened closely.

"Wish that Joe had never sucked my cock. Why am I looking at Butch like he's hot? The kid's nineteen and I am losing my mind."

Gay? You're a gay cowboy? Charlie!

Roman was about to scramble out of the bramble and call out to him but he felt it coming. He had learned now. The crow this time. *No. No!*

"Okay, boys. Let's head in for the night." Charlie spurred on a chestnut brown horse and galloped down the hillside.

Roman flapped as hard as he could and became airborne. He followed Charlie at a distance to watch him. A wonderful ranch house, over fifty horses, men working to keep them fed and clean, and a cabin where Charlie lived alone down a winding path in the woods.

Roman perched outside his window at night, watching him undress for bed or read. Alone. Every night. A man as beautiful as Charlie.

The more he watched, the more he learned. Charlie was sensitive, intelligent, and struggling with his new sexual awakening. The other men respected him, especially the older one called Vernon.

Charlie Mosby, you are who I need. You are the one.

Chapter 10

"Charlie?"

He raised his head from his palm to see Suzie standing in front of his table. Three beers in him and no food, Charlie was just beginning to feel a slight buzz.

"Can I sit down?"

He used his boot to push out the chair for her but didn't want her to join him.

Instead of choosing the chair across from him, she moved his hat aside and sat adjacent to him. Scooting closer, she rubbed his back affectionately. "Butch is an ass. We all know that."

"I did wrong. I did wrong by Vernon." Charlie tried to sit up in his chair, tipping the last drop of beer onto his tongue from an empty glass.

"Dad loves you like a son."

"Not no more." He rubbed his face. "Where's my manners. Let me buy you a drink."

"Thanks, Charlie. Just white wine, please."

He nodded, standing up and walking to the bar. "Wine and another beer." He put cash on the counter. The bartender handed him two glasses. "Keep the change," Charlie said, carrying the drinks back to the table.

"Thank you." Suzie took her stemmed glass from him.

"You're welcome." Charlie sat back down and sipped his fresh beer. "So? What did your mom and pop say? Hm? Are they going to fire me?"

"No. I don't think so. I think Dad was surprised. Like we all were."

Charlie covered his eyes with one hand in embarrassment.

"Don't worry. We all love and support you."

"Suzie, I don't even know what I am yet." He leaned his elbows on the table. "I… This fella, he's…he's…"

"Your boyfriend?"

"No. I mean. He's the first, well, second man…I mean, I didn't go with another man before him. I just…" He shook his head. "Never mind. I can't spit out the gory details. I'm a gay boy. There. I admitted it."

"And you can be gay. It's okay."

"No. It ain't okay to do what I did out in the open. That kind of thing is for the bedroom. I know that. It's just…just this guy…this fella, he's…"

"Gorgeous?" she laughed as she replied.

Charlie smiled at her silly giggle.

"Like wow!" She fanned herself. "Where did you guys meet?"

"Suzie Norman, I cannot believe how well you are taking this."

"Charlie!" She whacked his shoulder playfully. "Sherlane and I are going to college in the big city now. We meet all kinds of people. Dad didn't teach us to hate nobody."

"No. He did a good job raising you two." Charlie squeezed her hand. Just then, he noticed a man standing near them. Charlie leapt to his feet and gaped at Roman, who was wearing his clothing, and everything was tight on the big man.

Suzie spun around to look.

"Charlie…we need to talk." Roman appeared very nervous, and Charlie knew why.

"Join us." Suzie gestured to the open chair. "Don't be afraid. Charlie, introduce me."

"Suzie, this is Roman." Charlie walked closer to Roman, who wasn't wearing shoes, just in stocking feet. "What the hell are you doin'?" he asked privately. "You change into a wolf or crow in here and them good ole boys will be on you with pool sticks."

"I'll be able to feel it coming. And damn, I would love a beer." He licked his lips.

"Sit." Charlie pointed to the vacant seat.

"Hey. I'm no dog. So don't talk to me like I'm one." Roman sat down. "I'm not one at the moment anyway."

Charlie raced to the bar, having no idea how little time Roman had as a human. "Beer, please." He put a few dollars on the counter and looked at Suzie and Roman getting acquainted. "Thanks." He practically ran back to the table with the beer, sloshing it as he set it down.

"Slow down, Charlie," Suzie said, "I just told Roman what Butch did. But he said he already knows."

"You okay, Charlie?" Roman reached for his hand.

"None of that in here. You kiddin' me?" Charlie drew his hand back.

"Charlie, it's okay." Suzie took one of each their hands and brought them together in front of her. "I'm hiding it." She placed both her hands on top of theirs.

"I knew you were the sweet one." Roman smiled.

"Sherlane is too. I'm just more assertive." Suzie grinned. "Grr, you sure are a pretty man, Roman."

"Did she just growl?" Roman laughed, sipping his beer. "Mm, oh man, did I miss a glass of cold beer."

"Where did you go that there wasn't any beer?"

"Anyway..." Charlie interrupted and took his hand back from the group clasp. "How long have you got, Roman?"

"Isn't that your shirt, Charlie?" Suzie touched the flannel at Roman's sleeve. "Oh, honey, these don't fit you well. Look. The button holes are gapping. But how cute that you want to wear each other's clothing."

Roman didn't comment on Suzie's observation. "I don't know, Charlie. But I did know Butch shook you up and I needed to see you."

"It'd be easier if you waited at the cabin." Charlie tilted his head at Suzie. "How'd you get here?"

"Hitched a ride on one of your wranglers' trucks. Your boys dropped me here."

Charlie slouched in his chair, rubbing his face in exhaustion. "So, all the help knows I like cock. That's just great."

"Babe."

"Charlie, it's okay," Suzie said.

"No. It ain't." Charlie pushed his chair out, took his hat and jacket, and left. As he walked to his truck in the parking lot, he heard the noises behind him. Charlie spun around to see first Roman then Suzie hurrying after him.

When Roman tried to stop him, Charlie shoved him off.

"I can't even figure myself out yet, Roman. How am I going to deal with helping you? I have to work with them boys at the ranch. How will I do that?"

Suzie caught up to them. "Calm down, both of you."

"I need some time. I can't do all this at once." Charlie climbed into his truck.

Roman grabbed him, not allowing him to shut the door. "Don't abandon me, Charlie. I'm desperate for help, and I need you. Please."

"I know. And I'm sorry. But my whole life just got shook out of whack today, and how do I help you when I can't even see through my own mess? You understand?"

"Baby…" Roman touched his hair.

Charlie felt an emotional lump in his throat. "Don't use that card now." Charlie glanced at Suzie quickly. He mouthed silently to Roman, *"Not the sex thing."*

"Who else can I turn to? Who else?" Roman begged with his watery eyes.

Of Wolves and Men

Suzie said, "Charlie Mosby, how can you be so mean? I'm here for you, Roman. I'll drive you home if he's too stubborn to."

Charlie was about to say something when he took a look at Roman's expression. "Oh no."

Roman cringed and held onto the truck door frame.

"What's wrong?" Suzie stepped nearer. "Roman? Are you okay?"

"Suzie, go back to the ranch. I'll take care of this," Charlie said.

"Of what?" She raised her hands in a questioning gesture. "Is he sick?"

"Get in. *Get in!*" Charlie grabbed Roman and ushered him to the passenger's side of his truck. Roman moaned and doubled over. Charlie reached around to hold him from behind. "Fight it, baby, fight it."

"I can't." Roman's voice got swallowed down into a whimper.

"I'm sorry for thinkin' of myself. I'll help you. I don't know how, but I'll try." He gripped Roman as tightly as he could and felt his body changing right under his grasp.

Roman dropped to all fours next to the truck.

Charlie heard a high pitched gasp and looked up to see Suzie's eyes growing wide. "I told you to go!"

The clothing began slipping off Roman and he growled as he shook his furry body.

"Don't get hit by a car, Roman. Get in the truck."

Roman spun around, breaking out of Charlie's grip, the transformation complete. His eyes were pure green and lit up from the ambient lights. He showed his teeth and bolted across the busy main street in front of the bar, vanishing into the tree line.

Charlie looked down at the pile of clothing at his feet.

He heard a noise and saw Suzie holding onto the fender, shaking. Charlie held her in his arms as she got over what she had seen. "Okay. Okay, Suzie." He rocked her, calming her.

"Poor man. I can't believe it. I understand why you were so against the leg traps, Charlie."

"You can't tell a soul, Suzie. Please."

"No one would believe me."

"I don't know how this happened to him or how to help him."

Suzie released her hold on Charlie and picked up the clothing. "If I hadn't seen it with my own eyes..." She trembled as she folded the shirt.

"Not a word." He held up his finger.

"Not a word." Suzie set the clothing down on the passenger's seat of the truck. "Did he say how?"

"He thinks it was a Ute shaman."

"How's that possible?"

"You're askin' me?" Charlie shook his head and looked back in the direction Roman had run. "I don't know where to begin findin' out how to fix him."

"Let me head back to the ranch. I have my laptop there. We can at least do a little research."

Charlie grabbed her hand. "I can't thank you enough."

"I had no idea...really. No idea any of this was possible."

"I still think I'm seeing things. But if it's bad for us, how does Roman feel?"

"I can't imagine."

"I'll meet you back at my cabin, okay?"

"Yes. I'll meet you there."

Charlie watched her walk to her car. He sat behind the wheel of the truck and followed her home.

~

Roman ran on through the woods in the direction of the ranch. Though he was in good shape as a man, having the stamina of a timber wolf was incredible. Using his sense of smell to guide him, Roman cut through the dense underbrush, stopping only at roadways so he didn't end up road-kill. He trotted across a four lane highway quickly and kept making progress towards the ranch. He caught a strong musky scent and then the sound of something following him. He wheeled around and had a look, panting, his tongue hanging out of his mouth. His sense of smell caught it before his ears and eyes. A coyote was staring at him. Female.

Get lost. He continued his journey to the ranch, hearing the female tracking him and not sure why or what to do about it. He didn't want a dog fight. Other scents caught up to him. Territory. That was it. He was crossing another marked area where he had not been before on four legs.

The noise behind him grew louder. He looked back to see the female coyote snapping at his heels.

You have to be kidding me! Roman faced her, showing his teeth. *Look, lady, I'm bigger and meaner than you, and I'm just passing through. So go away!*

She took a bold snap at him.

He felt the hair rise on his back and exposed his teeth. A game of stalemate began and the female coyote circled him, sniffing and licking her nose.

He caught a very strong odor and felt his stomach churn. *Please tell me you're not a bitch in heat. Honey, I'm gay in any shape. And I'm not mounting you.*

Her menacing circling and body language became softer, less threatening and more courtship. Roman resumed his pace to the ranch, but had a feeling his suitor wouldn't give up easily. He had no idea how to rebuff a female coyote. It was easy for him when he was human. *Sorry, but I'm gay.* Can he tell that she-coyote the same thing?

The distraction of having her literally on his tail, snapping at his hind legs, was pissing him off. He did a one-eighty spin and bit her on the snout. She yelped but was not put off easily.

As he stood still, she sniffed at his back end. Roman didn't want to hurt her, but he certainly didn't want her hanging around. Her cold nose touched under his tail. He leapt up and gave her another snapping of his jaws. She immediately lay on her back in a submissive pose, pawing at his chest.

Go away! Find a coyote and not a man in wolf-drag!

Roman wasn't happy about this waste of time. If he changed into a man now, it'd be a long walk. Being a crow at this moment would be helpful, but no matter how hard he tried, he couldn't control the changes.

With his coyote shadow nipping at his bottom as he ran, Roman caught the scent of the horses on the ranch. He knew he was getting close as familiar smells of the surrounding woods came to his sharp senses.

He slowed down and stood still, ears perked up. Charlie and Suzie were back, their vehicles parked in the lot in front of the ranch house. He peered over his shoulder and the female coyote was behind him, looking as she had staked her claim over him.

This is the last place you want to be, sweetie. These cowboys will trap, shoot, and skin you. Since aggression did nothing, Roman nudged her with his nose to go away. He didn't know doggie language for 'Get lost'. He had no idea how to tell her she was in danger.

She stood beside him, licking his ear and mouth.

Stop. That tickles. Come on. Go away. He pointed his nose downward and used the top of his head to push her back. She didn't budge. Roman dropped to the ground to think things out, lying down and keeping his eyes on the action at the ranch.

She kept sniffing at him. Maybe his mixture of scents was confusing her. She stood over him, a paw on either side.

You dry hump me, bitch, and I'll get violent. Roman looked into her eyes. *Can't you see what I am? Come on. Go find a real mate.*

Of Wolves and Men

Something startled her and she bolted into the woods. Roman stayed put, listening.

Suzie was holding a laptop, talking a mile a minute to Charlie, who was nodding his head as he walked to the cabin.

Roman stood and made his way towards them slowly. They entered Charlie's cabin, turning on lights and closing the door. Roman put his front paws on the window ledge and watched.

Suzie set her computer on the coffee table, sitting on the floor beside it, while Charlie headed to the kitchen.

Roman could hear their conversation easily. Suzie was discussing how she and Charlie needed to speak to someone from the Ute tribe to see if they knew of any shaman's curse.

Good girl. Roman gave the area a glance and noticed JP and Goat heading down the path to their cabin. Roman vanished into the woods until they passed. A cold nose made him nearly jump out of his fur. Roman stayed still, sensing the coyote do the same next to him, as the men came closer, chatting about Charlie and his oral sex with a man on the trail. The way they laughed at Charlie angered Roman. He showed his fangs and became enraged. Charlie needed their support, not to be the butt of their jokes.

Just as they passed and Roman's anger piqued he began to feel a change coming on. He shivered and lay on his back on the ground. Clenching his teeth to keep his moans of pain behind them, Roman rode out the agony of his body shifting shape. The coyote was licking him, as if she knew he was injured or sick. As Roman morphed into a man, he shivered and covered his crotch with his hand. "You happy now?" he whispered to the coyote. "I'm a guy. Go find a canine to fuck."

Even in coyote language Roman could see she was terrified. Her ears went back and she bolted away into the darkness of the woods.

"Ew." Roman raised his hand from his crotch. "That was seriously disgusting." He slowly managed to get to his feet, holding onto tree trunks for balance. After making sure the coast was clear, he grabbed the doorknob of Charlie's cabin, turned it and entered. Suzie nearly jumped out of her skin in surprise as Charlie returned with two cups of coffee from the kitchen. "Welcome back."

"I need a shower. Bad." Roman covered his crotch and walked to the bathroom.

~

"Be right back, Suzie." Charlie followed behind Roman as he turned on the water. "Poor baby."

"You don't want to touch me at the moment. Believe me." Roman stepped into the tub and scrubbed the soap all over his body, especially his crotch.

"Why? What did you get into? A cow pie?"

"Worse."

"I asked Suzie to give us a hand. I mean, the cat's out of the bag to her."

"Can we trust her?" Roman shut off the water and Charlie handed him a towel.

"What choice do we have? She saw it all." Charlie glanced down at Roman's cock and low hanging balls. "Literally."

"I'm losing my mind, Charlie. I have to get out of this stupid curse." He rubbed the towel over his head while Charlie used a second one on his back.

"Let me get you something to wear meanwhile. Seeing you naked would give anyone a hard-on. Including Suzie."

"Do you have sweatpants? Getting into your jeans was nearly impossible."

"I do. Stay put."

"Sit. Stay." Roman exhaled loudly. "Getting a cold, wet snout in the balls. What more can they do to me?"

"Huh?"

"Nothing. Go."

Of Wolves and Men

Charlie didn't even want to ask. He left Roman and dug through his drawers, returning with a pair of sweatpants and a t-shirt.

When he entered the bathroom to give it to Roman, he was pinned against the wall and kissed. Charlie grunted at the surprise and dropped the clothing. Roman gnawed up Charlie's neck to his jaw. Charlie was going to mention Suzie in the next room but Roman's touch was too arousing to stop. "Will this turn you back?"

"I fucking hope not. I'm done being a dog for the night." Roman unfastened Charlie's belt and then his button and zipper. He exposed Charlie's cock from his clothing and kissed him.

Charlie held onto Roman tightly, deepening the kiss as his length was fondled and tugged. Roman held both their cocks upright together, and fisted them. Charlie broke the kiss. "Oh, I gotta see this." He looked downwards, widening his stance for balance. Both of them watched as Roman used two hands to jerk them off.

Charlie was soon coated in sweat and gasping for breath. The sight of their dicks pressed side by side and being given a hand-job was too good to be true. "I'm there," he said, squeezing Roman's shoulders. Roman increased the tightness of his grip and the speed of his fisting. Charlie's cum sprayed out like a fountain of cream, running down Roman's knuckles. Roman's cock erupted a second later, adding to the oozing cum. With the semen as lube, Roman gave both of their dicks a slow massage. Charlie cupped Roman's head and opened his mouth, sucking on Roman's tongue as he panted and recuperated.

"Uh. Guys?"

Charlie backed up from Roman's kiss. "Yeah, Suzie?" Charlie grabbed a towel and handed it to Roman.

"The shamans from Ute are only healers and they don't call them shamans. You sure about the tribe, Roman?"

"No. I'm not sure about anything." Roman washed his hands and dragged the sweatpants up his legs as Charlie tucked himself into his jeans.

"We'll be right out, Suzie. Sorry." Charlie straightened his shirt and handed Roman the t-shirt. "That was so good." He pecked Roman's lips. "I have got to get you straight, 'cause I want that every day."

"It isn't good because I'm straight, babe." Roman's smiled wryly.

"You know what I mean." Charlie checked his appearance in the mirror quickly then asked, "We ready?"

"As we can be."

He opened the door and found Suzie sitting on the floor cross-legged, sipping from her cup of coffee. "What do you know about the incident, Roman?" she asked.

"You want a cup?" Charlie pointed to the coffee mug.

"No, but I'm starving. You have any food?"

"I'll find something for you." Charlie headed to the kitchen, listening to Roman as he spoke.

~

Roman sat on the sofa and ran his hand through his damp hair. "I remember a woman's face. It was painted red with white and blue stripes."

"The shaman legends are mostly from eastern Europe." Suzie sipped more coffee. "The local tribes have medicine people, but I'm not seeing anything from the Indian Nations that could turn you into something not human." Suzie scrolled down the computer screen.

"Can I have a stab at it? I have a little research experience." Roman caught the scent of eggs frying and heard his stomach grumble.

"Sure." Suzie scooted over.

Of Wolves and Men

Roman picked up the computer. When was the last time he had access to one. And a phone! "Charlie!" His unexpected shout scared Suzie and she jumped.

"What?" Charlie rushed into the room, a plate and spatula in his hand. "You changin'? You need me to open the door?"

"Can I borrow your cell phone?" Roman held out his hand.

"In my coat pocket. Over there." Charlie walked back to the stove. "Your omelet's done."

"Thanks, babe." Roman dug through Charlie's pockets and removed the cell phone, he flipped it open and paused to remember Phil's number. Rubbing his face, he struggled. He held up the phone and punched in the numbers, putting it to his ear. A loud metallic tone sounded, then a recorded message, "The number you have reached has been disconnected...if you feel—" Roman ended the call and thought harder. "What was it...what was it?" His head ached. He turned to Suzie. "Can you look up the ATF office number in Reno?"

"They have it online?" She sat in front of the computer again.

"Yes. They have a website with field office numbers."

Charlie brought a plate to the table. "Hash browns and a western omelet."

"Smells great." Roman sat in a chair at the table and began devouring the food.

"There's a Reno phone number in a field office, a satellite office..." Suzie said.

"The field office number." Roman stuffed food into his mouth, barely chewing he was so hungry. As Suzie read the numbers, Roman used his thumb to dial. He looked up. Charlie was watching him eat. "Tastes great. Thanks." Roman put the phone to his ear as it rang.

"ATF, can I help you?"

"Can you connect me with Agent Phil Dean's extension? I can't remember it."

"Agent Phil Dean?"

"Yes." Roman took another mouthful of food.

"Hold one moment."

Roman ate the last bite off the plate and used his finger to wipe the rest, licking it off.

Charlie handed him a napkin. "Another helping?"

"I would love one, but no. I'm good for now." Roman tapped his fingers. "I can't believe I'm on hold. What the hell? Why didn't they transfer me to Phil's voicemail?"

"Who's Phil?"

Roman glanced up at Charlie's pout. "Get over here, cowboy." Roman tugged Charlie to his lap and rubbed his face in his shirt.

"Wow." Suzie blushed.

"He's an animal." Charlie laughed, holding onto Roman with his arm around his shoulder. "Figuratively and literally."

"Hello?" Roman said into the phone. "Come on, come on…"

"Who are you trying to call?"

"One of the other agents that was on that incident with me. Phil Dean. He and I were searching—"

"Hello?" the woman on the phone said.

"Yes." Roman sat up. "I'm holding for Agent Phil Dean."

"He no longer works out of this office. Can I ask why you are calling and redirect your call?"

"How about the field supervisor, Nick Hoffman?"

"May I ask who's calling?"

Roman looked into Charlie's eyes. He cupped the phone. "She's asking my name. What should I do?"

"The ATF agent is asking me?" Charlie laughed softly.

"Shit." Roman replied to her, "This is Roman Burk. Special Agent Roman Burk."

"Did you say, Roman Burk?"

He swallowed hard as his throat went dry. Was it possible that everyone knew he went missing? "Yes."

"Hold on while I transfer you."

Of Wolves and Men

Roman wanted to talk to Phil. How would he explain what happened to anyone else? His stress level began to rise and with it came anger and frustration. "Oh fuck no!" Roman began feeling a change coming.

Charlie held him in both arms. "Hang in there, Roman…"

Suzie jumped to her feet. "Is it happening again?"

"Yeah." Charlie moved off of Roman's lap.

"Hello?" a voice said from over the phone line, "Roman? Roman Burk is that you?"

Roman recognized his supervisor's voice but couldn't answer him. He dropped the phone and doubled over.

~

Charlie shouted to Suzie, "Get that door open. We don't want to be cooped up in here with a wolf." While Suzie opened the door, Charlie asked Roman, "Should I pick up the phone? What should I do?"

Roman dropped to his knees on the floor, curling up into a ball from the pain.

Charlie crouched beside him and picked up the cell phone. He put it to his ear. "Hello?" The line was dead. He looked at the LCD screen and was about to ask if he should redial when he heard a loud squawk. The big black crow was shaking its feathers and flapping its wings on the floor beside him. Charlie sank down next to him and leaned against the leg of the kitchen table. "How am I going to help you?" Charlie rubbed his face tiredly. "What am I supposed to do?"

Suzie closed the door and knelt beside them. "He's a crow too?"

Roman bounced around the wood flooring before hopping onto one of Charlie's legs.

Charlie felt the sharp talons through his blue jeans. The clothing Roman had worn was again just a pile on the floor.

With his eyes burning with tears, Charlie said to Suzie, "I have no idea what to do."

Suzie scooted closer and held Charlie for comfort.

G. A. Hauser

Charlie stared into Roman's black eye as he stared back.

Chapter 11

"Charlie?" JP knocked.

Charlie gently nudged Roman off his leg and hurried to the door. He poked his head out. "What is it, JP?"

"Vernon sent me to get you. He wants to talk to you."

"All right."

"Is Suzie in there too? Connie wants to know if she'll be helping prepare dinner."

"I'm here, JP." Suzie stood beside Charlie. "Tell Mom I'm heading back now."

"Okay." JP nodded and walked down the path.

Once he closed the door, Charlie looked at Roman who was still perched on the floor tilting his head at them. "Do you want to go outside?" he asked Roman.

Roman shook his head and flapped.

"Is that a no?" Suzie asked.

"I think so. I can't tell." Charlie crouched down. "Make one noise for yes, two for no."

Roman let out a loud caw sound.

"Okay. Stay here. It'll be warmer if you change back again. And if you do, here's the phone." Charlie placed it on the table. "Suzie will leave her computer for now. Okay?"

Roman let out another loud squawk.

"Right. Here comes the moment of truth." Charlie put his hat and coat on. "When your dad fires me."

"He's not going to fire you." Suzie slipped on her coat.

"Sure he ain't." Charlie glanced back at Roman. "You sure you'll be okay?"

Roman flapped his wings and made another noise.

Charlie sighed loudly and left, locking the door behind him. He didn't need anyone coming in and finding Roman in any form.

He and Suzie walked in the cold air up the path to the ranch house, their breath making vapor clouds as they moved. Inside, the fireplace was keeping the living area warm and JP, Goat, and Sherlane were all sipping coffee together. They stopped talking when Charlie and Suzie entered. Harley raced over and began sniffing Charlie's leg and boots. Charlie figured he could smell Roman on him.

"All right, dog. Enough smelling." He nudged him away and Harley trotted to the kitchen where Connie was busy making supper.

Charlie tipped his cap in greeting to Sherlane. "Vernon in his office?"

"Yeah," Goat said, staring at Charlie as if he had sprouted horns.

Suzie gave his arm a reassuring squeeze, then joined her mother and Sherlane in the kitchen.

Charlie removed his hat and held it by his side. "Ya there, boss?" He tilted his head near the office door.

"Come on in, Charlie."

After taking a deep breath to face the inevitable, Charlie entered the room.

"Have a seat."

He tossed his hat on another chair and plopped down heavily.

A moment past and Charlie and Vernon assessed each other in that silence.

"You're like a son to me."

"I'm sorry, Vernon…"

Vernon interrupted him. "Let me finish."

Nodding, Charlie lowered his head.

Of Wolves and Men

"I am surprised by what happened with that other man. Roman, someone said his name was."

Charlie met Vernon's eyes. "Roman Burk."

"Fine." Vernon shifted in his seat. "I think you two playing like that where some of our patrons could see you was wrong."

"Yes, sir." Charlie knew finding another job without Vernon as a reference was going to be tough.

"But if you promise me it won't happen again…"

He perked up. "I promise."

"When I… Charlie…I thought you and my girls had…" Vernon cleared his throat. "Was I mistaken to think you were attracted to one of them?"

Charlie shifted in his chair. Months ago he was considering making a move on one if he could do it without making the other jealous. Last time they showed up, he was trying to decide which sister to begin dating. He knew he had Vernon and Connie's blessing. How does one explain that a blowjob from a man that helped him change a flat tire on the freeway swayed his thinking; opened up options, and began a bi-curious interest in him?

"I'm just not real comfortable talking about this yet, boss. This is all so new to me too. And I don't know what I want."

"All right, Charlie. But you just know either way, you got Connie and my support."

"Then I'm not fired?"

"No. No, son. Not as long as you keep that kind of thing private."

"Yes, sir." Charlie felt his cheeks blush at the mistake. But with Roman, you either took advantage of the man when he was human, or you lost out. *That* fact he was not going to explain. "What about Butch?"

"Yes. What about Butch?" Vernon sat up in his chair. "I gave you a pass for bad behavior. I'm going to give him one."

"Yes, sir." Charlie knew that was fair.

"But you two boys need to sit face to face and work this out. I don't want any friction out there on the ranch."

"I couldn't agree more."

"Right. That's enough on the topic. How about we go socialize while the girls cook us dinner?" Vernon stood from the chair and walked around the desk. He handed Charlie his hat from where it was on a second chair. "Everything taken care of with the horses for the night?"

"I'll have to ask the boys. I've been…well…" Charlie took his hat from Vernon.

"Preoccupied." Vernon patted his back.

"You have no idea." Charlie opened the door and they walked down the hall to the living room.

"You can invite your friend, Charlie. We'd all like to get to know him. Is he local?"

"No." Charlie stopped when he noticed Butch sitting with JP and Goat.

"Use my office, Charlie." Vernon pointed at Butch. "You go and have a talk with Charlie in private."

Butch looked pained. He stood and walked closer to Charlie. "May as well get this over with."

"Yeah. May as well." Charlie hung his hat on a rack with his coat and returned to Vernon's office, closing the door behind them. They both stood, arms crossed.

"So? You're a fag?"

"I don't know. I'm kind of lost at the moment."

"How can you suck a guy's dick?"

Charlie shrugged. "I don't know. I guess it sounded bad a few months ago. It isn't so bad now."

"Not so bad?" Butch made a face of revulsion.

"All right, let's not get into all that. Vernon wants us to just manage to work together. Can we do that?"

"I ain't the one with the problem."

Charlie sat on the arm of a chair. "Oh? Cuttin' out a deer's heart ain't a problem?"

Of Wolves and Men

"That was just for nothing. It ain't like I do it all the time." Butch said, "You're the one with the new bad habit."

"I don't like it when you smirk at me, Butch Crowell. So don't be doin' that."

Butch touched his own zipper flap. "You want to suck my cock?"

"Not particularly. You want my fist in your face again?"

Butch smiled in a self-satisfied way. "I thought you took a shine to me when I first showed up for my interview."

Charlie felt his cheeks grow warm. No denying he did think that at first. But he hadn't met Roman yet. And a nineteen year old with bad judgment didn't compare to an older man with life experience. Even with Roman's 'unusual' problems.

"I thought you were a nice guy. Yes. That's why we hired you."

"Nice?" Butch closed the gap between them, leaning on Charlie's leg where he was propped on the arm of the chair.

~

Roman hopped on the wooden floor over to the computer, left open, on the coffee table. He stared at the screen and pecked at a key. It was useless.

The confinement of the cabin began wearing on his nerves. *How much longer am I going to be able to stand this?* He flapped his wings and hit the door deliberately, feet first, landing in front of it. He should have left with Charlie and Suzie. The reason he hadn't was he was tired of waking up naked in the woods, freezing his balls off.

He flapped his wings and clamped both his talons on the doorknob, but there was no way to turn it. Hopping and flapping, Roman made the rounds to see if there was a way out. Because of the cold, all the windows were shut tight. He was trapped for the moment. Waddling across the floor to the computer again, Roman looked at the screen. The website with the ATF phone numbers was still showing. He managed to stand beside the computer on the coffee table, using his beak to try and turn back to previous screens. The one Suzie had checked for Indian shaman's showed up. Roman jumped across the gap between the sofa and coffee table so he could read the information. No shamans in North America. It wasn't a Native American medicine person that did this to him, was it? No. Who was it?

Roman tried to recall the graffiti on the walls of that room. The inverted pentagram came to mind, but he knew it had been partially erased by newer tags. Was this satanic? What was the significance of a wolf and a crow? There was nothing in this deed that struck him as demonic. It still had all the signs of a tribal curse. An earth worshipping cult? Witches? Maybe if he included the sacrifice of the animals he had encountered, and the use of strange drugs to put him into a sedated state he could come to that conclusion. Witch craft. The blood painted all over his body…

A stab of pain hit him as he became enraged about the deed.

Roman felt it coming. He backed up against the couch cushions and buried his beak in his wing, preparing for the agony.

~

"Why are you behavin' like this with me, Butch?" Charlie nudged him away.

"Cuz you an' me are supposed to be repairing our relationship."

Both he and Butch jolted at a noise of rapping on the window of Vernon's office.

"Charlie!"

"Roman!" Charlie pushed Butch aside to get closer to the window. He yanked up the blinds and held back the curtains.

"Don't go with him, Charlie, please!"

"I'm not." Charlie glanced over his shoulder at Butch, who seemed glad he was causing friction. Leaning closer to the window, Charlie could see Roman in the sweatpants and t-shirt he had lent him. "Hang on. Let me come out there."

"Where did you meet that guy, Charlie? He seems like he's an unemployed waster."

"Don't start," Charlie said, pointing his finger at Butch. He left the office and rushed through the house.

"What's wrong, Charlie?" Vernon was standing near the fireplace, a beer in his hand.

"Nothin'. Just got to check on somethin'." He removed his hat and coat from the rack.

"His man-friend is banging on the window trying to get in," Butch said, that smirk back on his face.

"Invite him in, Charlie. He's welcome." Vernon gestured with his beer, trying to make Charlie feel comfortable.

"Thanks, Vernon. But I don't know." Charlie glanced at Butch and left. He met up with Roman at the side of the ranch house. "What are you doing?" Charlie gripped Roman's arm.

"I can see you two staring at each other. Don't go with him, Charlie."

"I never even seen a woman as possessive as you."

"Sorry..." Roman rubbed his face and hair. "I've never been like this with anyone before. I think it's the alpha wolf in me."

"You want to give dinner a try? Or?"

"In there?" Roman pointed to the ranch house.

"They said you're welcome. It's just a matter of...you know."

"Yeah. You know." Roman threw up his hands in frustration, pacing. "I can't. I know what'll happen. And that Butch asshole, he gets on my nerves."

"I know. I'll bring a plate back to the cabin for you." Charlie touched Roman's face. "I won't go out on you. Not with no one. You got that?"

Roman embraced Charlie roughly. He kissed his neck and squeezed him tight. "I don't know where I'd find another man like you. I need you."

"I know, babe." Charlie hugged him back, feeling him shiver. "You need to get inside the cabin. Should I come with you and make sure the fire is keeping the place warm?"

"I can manage until…"

"I know."

"And your phone rang while I was still a crow. I couldn't answer it, but my guess?"

Charlie touched the dark growth of hair on Roman's jaw affectionately.

"It's the ATF trying to trace that call I made to them and figure out whose number it is. After all, I'm a missing person now."

"Why didn't they stay on the line? I would have talked to them."

"They probably wanted to do a reverse number check or it may have just gotten cut off accidentally." Roman looked out the long winding drive. "Don't be surprised if you get a visit from them."

"What should I tell them?"

"Tell them what happened to me. If I'm human, I will. I feel sick about my family. They must think I was kidnapped and left for dead."

"Call them. Go use my phone." Charlie nudged Roman.

"I can't. If my mom answers and I can't talk because I'm turning into something…" Roman appeared tired. "She'll just get more upset. I have to figure out what to do first."

"I can talk to anyone you need me to."

"Charlie?" Suzie called from the door. "Oh, hi, Roman. Are you going to try and join us?"

"Hi. I doubt it. When a timber wolf is sitting at the table, that won't go over too well with the rest of the family, will it?"

"Let me make up a plate of food for you."

Of Wolves and Men

When Suzie went back inside, Charlie asked, "Do you want me to speak to your family?"

Roman cupped Charlie's face tenderly. "I appreciate it. But they wouldn't believe you. They'd think you were a nut job."

Suzie returned with a plastic container of food. "Here you go."

"Thanks, Suz..."

"Let me get a plate and go back to the cabin and eat with you." Charlie made a move towards the house.

"No. You eat with the family. It's okay." Roman pecked his lips and walked down the path to his cabin.

Charlie and Suzie waited until he vanished from sight.

"I can't stand seeing him like that." Charlie shook his head. "What are we going to do? Since that shaman idea didn't pan out, I don't have a clue."

"Come inside. It's cold." Suzie held the door open for Charlie but he allowed her to go first.

"Where's your boyfriend?" Butch asked.

"Don't you say it like that." Charlie pointed his finger. "I swear, Butch, I won't put up with taunting."

"What'd I say?" He acted innocent.

Vernon waved the men into the kitchen. "Go eat. Connie has it on the table." Vernon waited for the rest of the men to leave the living room and approached Charlie. "I take it he doesn't feel welcome."

"No. It's not that." Charlie met gazes with Suzie before she joined the rest of the group in the kitchen. "Make up a plate for me, Suzie."

"I will, Charlie."

He asked Vernon, "Boss, you ever hear of the Indian tribes practicing any black magic type or things in this area?"

"No. Quite the opposite. The tribes here have nothing to do with black arts. Why?"

"Just somethin' Roman and I were discussin', that's all. So? That cut up deer?"

"That's some satanic cult. There ain't no way that's got to do with the nations."

"And how do I figure out which cult is doing that?" Charlie gestured in the direction where he had found the cut fence and deer.

"Be best if you talk to the sheriff's department. I don't know who else. That's the first incident I've heard of in these parts."

Suzie brought him a plastic sectioned plate with a foil cover. "Here you go, Charlie. Should I stop by after dinner to help you with the research?"

Vernon looked intrigued. "You're looking deeper into this, Charlie? I felt since it was only one deer, and that's it, that they had moved on."

Charlie put on his hat and coat, opening the front door. "No sense in not bein' careful." Charlie thanked Suzie for the food. "I'll call you if we can't figure it out."

"Okay," Suzie replied.

"If you need the computer, just holler." Charlie stepped outside.

"You can borrow it. I know Sherlane has one."

Hearing the sound of tire on gravel, Charlie glanced down the long driveway as two vehicles approached. "Son of a bitch, he was right." He raced to the cabin shouting for Roman.

Vernon yelled, "Who are they, Charlie?"

"ATF agents! Tell 'em to hang on!" Charlie pushed back the door of his cabin. The sweatpants and t-shirt were in a pile on the floor and the plate of food was eaten and left beside it, obviously by an animal. "Oh, hell no!" He put his own plate down on the kitchen table and raced around his cabin. "Roman!" He ran outside peering through the darkness. "Shee-it! Roman! The agents are here!" Charlie had no idea what they would think of his explanation.

Of Wolves and Men

When Charlie heard the low murmur of men talking as they approached, he wondered how much Vernon would be able to take of this new problem. It kept getting worse.

The two agents were trailed by the entire household, all curious to see what was going on.

"Are you Charlie Mosby?" One of the men showed his ID and badge. "I'm special agent Nick Hoffman, and this is agent Phil Dean. We're both with the ATF."

"Yes, sir." Charlie removed his hat.

"We need to speak to you."

"I know, sir."

Charlie gestured to his cabin. The two men entered, immediately looking at the floor and the pile of clothing and empty plate. Charlie rubbed his forehead and said to Vernon, "I'll fill you in later, all right? Can you get everyone back to the house for me?"

"Okay, Charlie. Are you in any sort of trouble?"

"I don't know. I don't think so." He caught even Butch looking concerned as he stood behind the women.

"Come on, folks. Let's go back to the house." Vernon corralled them, making sure no one hung behind to eavesdrop.

Charlie took a deep breath and closed the door. "Have a seat, gentlemen. Can I get you anythin'? Coffee?"

"We're fine." Agent Hoffman removed a pad from his suit pocket. "We traced a cell phone number back to you and this location."

"I know, sir." Charlie sat down. The men didn't. Agent Dean walked around the cabin checking it out.

"Since November first we've been looking for a missing agent." Agent Hoffman finally sat across from Charlie. The open laptop was sitting in front of him on the coffee table.

"Yes, sir." Charlie shook off his jacket and ran his hand through his hair.

"You say that like you know something about it."

Charlie felt Agent Dean standing behind him. He looked up at him and said, "You were the guy Roman was tryin' to find."

"Where is Roman, Mr. Mosby?" Agent Dean came around the sofa and sat on the arm of a chair.

"He's close by. I just don't know what to say or do to convince you what's happened to him."

"Were you involved with his kidnapping?" Agent Hoffman asked.

"No, sir."

"You better tell us what you know from the beginning." Agent Dean appeared slightly menacing.

"I will, sir. I will do my best." Charlie cleared his throat. "But you're not goin' to believe a word of it."

"Give us a try." Agent Hoffman smiled but it wasn't a friendly gesture. More of a grimace.

"I…" Charlie cleared his throat. "I was up at the west edge of the ranch, repairin' our fence. Someone had cut through and killed a doe, messin' her up bad." There was no reaction. Charlie wished Roman would walk through that door a man and help him out. "Well, we brought the carcass to Doc McMurray—"

"What's this got to do with our missing agent?" Agent Dean leaned towards him, his jaw muscles twitching over his clenched teeth.

Charlie assumed he and Roman may have been close, judging by both men looking for the other.

"It does in a roundabout way."

"Cut to the chase. I don't have time for this."

Agent Hoffman made a slight wave of his hand at Agent Dean to calm him down. "Continue, Mr. Mosby."

"The doc said the killing of the doe was satanic or cultish in nature. The doe had her heart cut out." Charlie felt sweat bead on his top lip and wiped at it with the back of his hand. "It was soon after that incident I found Roman."

Of Wolves and Men

"Found him?" Agent Dean asked, "Found him dead?"

"No. No, sir. Naked and lyin' in the woods. He had blood on him, but no wound that I could see."

"What did you do with him? Did you take him to the hospital?" Agent Hoffman asked, scribbling notes.

"No, sir. He didn't want me to. Begged me not to."

Agent Dean immediately acted like he didn't believe it, blowing out a loud blast of air and shifting his posture on the arm of a chair.

"What date was this?"

"Last Monday, sir."

"What did you do with him?" Agent Dean asked sharply.

"I brought him here. I tried to keep him warm. I took care of him."

"Where is he now?" Agent Hoffman asked while Agent Dean began another look around the cabin.

"He comes and goes. I wish he were here now. He *was* here a minute ago. He ate that meal." Charlie pointed to the empty plate and clothing on the floor. "Right there, he was using my phone to call you." He waved at the computer. "He asked me and Suzie to find your website for the phone number just an hour ago. He called looking for you, Agent Dean. But he couldn't remember your number."

"You buying this?" Agent Dean made an expression of disbelief at Agent Hoffman.

"Mr. Mosby," Agent Hoffman spoke softly, "Agent Burk has been missing. He was kidnapped under very suspicious circumstances."

"He told me. Well, he wasn't kidnapped. He said a shaman changed him…" Charlie rubbed his jaw because he knew this would not go over well. "…into a wolf and a crow."

"I think we need to take him to the office, Hoff. This isn't getting us anywhere." He stood over Charlie and puffed up in anger. "Where'd you hide his body?"

"I wouldn't harm a hair on that beautiful man's head." Charlie met his eyes. "I'm right attached to him." He didn't know if Roman had explained his sexual preference to these men or not. "I want to help him."

"You can help Roman by telling us where he is being held captive." Agent Hoffman stood over Charlie as well.

"He's not being held." Charlie shook his head. "I knew no one would believe me." He spotted the clothing. "You see that?" They glanced briefly at the pile. "Roman was wearing that last time I saw him. Suzie handed him a plate of food. That plate."

"Go question the girl." Agent Hoffman tilted his head to Dean. Agent Dean stormed out, leaving the door ajar.

After he left, Charlie took a deep breath. "Sir, I know it's crazy. Believe me." Charlie pointed to the computer again. "Suzie and I were tryin' to help Roman figure out who cast a spell on him. He swore it was a female shaman from the Ute tribe. But Suzie said there were none. So, we got to lookin'—"

"Mr. Mosby."

Charlie held out his wrists. "Go on and arrest me. I know you want to. Go on."

"Did you kill or kidnap Agent Burk?"

Charlie's eyes burned with tears. "No. I love the man. I wouldn't hurt him."

"Can you bring me to him? Show me where he is?"

"I wish I could. You have no idea. He can't control the changes. They come on and the poor man is in agony."

"The changes?"

"Yeah. Crow to man, man to wolf, wolf to man…"

"Is that the story you're sticking to?"

"It's the truth, so help me God." Charlie crossed his finger over his chest.

The door moved.

Of Wolves and Men

Charlie expected to see the second agent. Instead, a long black beak and feathers appeared. "It ain't no good, Roman. He doesn't believe me."

The agent stood straight and said, "Are you trying to tell me that's Agent Burk? What do you think I am, an idiot?"

"No, sir." Charlie slouched over his lap in defeat.

~

Roman was angry with the way they were treating Charlie, but knew all he could do to help was flap and hop on the floor. *Poor Charlie. They think you have something to do with me vanishing. How did I get you into this mess?*

He flapped and squawked, trying to get his supervisor to pay attention. The man was staring at him like he wanted to swat him.

"Is that your bird?"

"No, sir. That's Roman Burk."

"You realize the more you lie, the more serious this becomes."

"I'm not lying, sir. If you wait long enough, you'll see Roman as a man or a wolf next. You have my word."

Roman pecked at Nick's shoe. *Listen to him, ya jerk!*

Nick nudged Roman away and backed up.

Charlie grew concerned and crouched down. "Don't hurt him. You hear me?"

"Take that thing outside. There's no way you're going to convince me that's Agent Burk."

"I tried, Roman."

I know, babe. Roman waddled over to Charlie and stood on his boot.

"Hoff?" Phil poked his head in. "I've got Suzanne Norman here, she's—" He blinked and asked, "What's with the bird?"

"Mr. Mosby says that's Agent Burk."

Roman dove at Phil and flapped against his chest. *It's me again, you moron! Remember the bird in the parking lot?*

"You better get that thing away from me, or I'll hurt it."

"Roman," Charlie said, hurrying towards him. "Please. They don't believe us."

Suzie poked her head in. "Yup. Told you. That's him."

"I'm getting the feeling this is just some nasty prank." Nick put his pad into his pocket.

Phil said, "Ms. Norman gave me the same cock and bull story that Mr. Mosby did."

Roman grew furious and pecked at Phil's shoe. *Hello? How stupid are you? Bird from incident where, me-Roman disappeared? Anyone home?* Roman tried to see if either of their thoughts were picking up on the memory of what he did the day he was changed. They were highly suspicious of Charlie and Suzie's motives at the moment. He could hear Nick thinking about arresting them on false reporting charges.

Phil! Phil! You remember. Come on. Roman used his talons to climb Phil's trousers. The man nearly jumped out of his skin and whacked Roman off.

"I said, take it easy!" Charlie rushed towards Roman and caressed his dark feathers.

"Oh, Roman." Suzie hurried over. "Are you okay?"

"You two are sick. How dare you play this kind of stunt?" Phil was breathing fire. "Do you know how well loved and respected Agent Burk was?"

"We love him too. Especially Charlie." Suzie sat next to Roman on the floor. "And Roman loves him."

"Suzie, we don't know what information Roman would prefer keepin' quiet." Charlie shook his head at her.

They know, Charlie. You tell them what we mean to each other. Roman tried to hug Charlie's leg with his wings.

"Look, Charlie. He's holding onto you." Suzie petted Roman's feathers.

"This is a waste of time." Phil ground his jaw. Roman could see the muscles in him tense.

Nick walked towards the door. "This investigation will remain open. And if you pull another stunt, like calling the field office and stating you're Roman Burk…"

It was me! Hello? Roman flapped over to Nick and tried to get his attention. *I called you. What is wrong with you guys? Have you ever seen a bird act this way? Come on, change me! Change me now!* Roman held his wings as wide as they would spread, hoping he'd turn into himself in front of them.

"I think Roman is trying to tell you it was him, sir."

"Let's go, Hoff. This is pathetic." Phil opened the door wider.

Get Dean's phone number! Roman hopped up and down in front of Charlie frantically. *Get his number!*

Charlie stared at him in confusion.

Roman flew to the table, picked up Charlie's cell phone with his feet and poked it into his chest.

Charlie got it. He took the phone and asked, "Agent Dean, can I have your office number? Roman couldn't remember it. That's why he had us look up the field office on the computer."

"I don't believe this." Phil threw up his hands.

Roman was growing just as angry. He flew up and pecked Phil in the head. *You idiot! Give him your number!*

"I'm about to shoot that bird." Phil covered his head with his arms, when the look on his face changed.

Roman landed on the floor in front of him, staring at him. *Yes. Remember now? Remember the bird at the scene everyone wanted to shoot?*

Phil took his card out of his pocket. "Here. This is my direct line." He handed the card to Charlie.

"He appreciates it. And I have no doubt you'll get a phone call from him…" Charlie looked at Roman. "Very soon. Right, Roman?"

Roman waddled over to Phil's foot and pecked his shoe. *I will call you the minute I have fingers, you dickhead.*

Phil stepped back from Roman, giving him a long look. Roman knew he was thinking things out. How can two crazy crows manage to appear in less than a week?

The agents left.

At his intense frustration of not being able to communicate, Roman began to feel something coming on. He waddled into a corner of the room and spread his wings, bracing himself.

"What's he doing?" Suzie asked.

"Changing. Shit!" Charlie hurried out of the cabin. "Wait! Agent Dean! Agent Hoffman!"

Roman knew this would not be good. He was turning wolf not man.

"Roman?" Suzie crouched beside him. "Does it hurt real bad?"

Yes. Roman opened his beak to gain air and heard his bird squawks turning into canine vocalizations.

"Uh oh," Suzie said as she backed up.

"He's turning into himself right now." Charlie sounded breathless as he convinced the agents to return.

Suzie hurried to the door and shook her head. "No, Charlie. He's not."

Roman faced the men at the door. The change complete he caught their scent and recognized Phil's cologne. He met Charlie's eyes. "Oh no." Charlie appeared pale.

Nick and Phil entered the room, stopping short at the sight of Roman.

Roman felt the hairs stand on his back and neck from his fear.

Phil unholstered his gun.

Charlie blocked his shot. "Don't. It's Roman. Don't even think about it."

"Now you're telling me Roman is that wolf?" Phil held the gun by his side.

Of Wolves and Men

"You see a crow?" Charlie waved around. "Magic! The crow is a big, black timber wolf."

"More like bullshit." Phil left the cabin in anger.

Nick warned Charlie, "This crap has got to stop. You're wasting our time and are very close to being arrested for false reporting."

Roman crept closer.

"Sir, I thought he would turn back into himself. I swear. If I knew he was goin' to turn wolf I'd—" Charlie spotted Roman stalking Nick from behind. "Uh. You may want to move away from the door, sir."

Nick spun around, his eyes wide in fear.

Roman lunged for the open space and between them and left the cabin, using his nose to quickly lock onto Phil. He leapt on his back from behind, knocking him to the gravel driveway by his SUV. Phil panicked and spun around under Roman's large paws. Roman snarled, showing his teeth.

Charlie, Suzie, and Nick closed the gap, staring in shock.

"Don't hurt him, Roman," Charlie said.

I don't want to hurt him. I want to knock some sense into him. Roman glanced back at Nick who had his hand on his holstered gun. Roman stared at Phil as he shivered under him. He gave Phil a lick under his jaw which shocked Phil. Phil winced as if he was going to get his face eaten off.

You taste good, babe.

Roman began lapping Phil's neck.

"What is this animal doing? Get him off me!" Phil tried to stop the licking.

Roman heard Charlie let out a loud exhale and Nick said, "So? Big deal. You tamed a wolf cub from birth. It's been done before, Mr. Mosby."

In order to keep Phil pinned down until he changed into a man, Roman lay on top of him, his paws on his shoulders, looking at his eyes. *You see me yet? You see me in here?*

"Please get him off me." Phil sounded nervous.

"Believe me. I can't tell Roman what to do." Charlie laughed softly.

Roman rested his head on Phil's chest. He had thought about Phil as a lover. But Phil was straight. And Roman wasn't the kind of man to pursue a dead end. Since they traveled so often together, Roman knew all about Phil's dreams of becoming a husband and father, and retiring at an early age.

"Is he going to sleep on me?" Phil kept his hands on the ground beside him.

"He knows you. And I think you're beginnin' to know who he is too," Charlie said.

You tell him, Charlie. Roman stuck his snout under Phil's arm and sniffed. *Mm. Nice.* He wriggled on Phil's body.

"This wolf is getting off on me!" Phil's eyes widened. "Roman? Is that you?"

Roman's ears perked up and he stared into Phil's eyes again. They connected and Roman felt a slight sense of hope. The thoughts in Phil's head were muddled, but he was beginning to question the possibility.

Roman licked his chin again.

Nick stood over them. "This is pathetic. Come on, Phil. We have to get back to the office. Get that beast off of you."

Roman snarled at Nick and he stepped back from the threat. Once his supervisor moved away, Roman rested his head on Phil again. In amazement, he felt Phil petting his fur.

"Is it you, Roman? Is this what happened to you that day?"

Roman made a squeaking noise because he'd tried to bark and couldn't.

"Fine. I'm not quite buying it yet, but how about one noise for yes, two for no. Okay?'

Roman glanced back at the other three who were watching closely.

In reply to Phil's initial query, Roman made one noise.

Phil looked at the others and then asked so only Roman could hear, "Are you gay?"

Roman pressed his paws harder into Phil and made a little noise, licking his chin again.

"Stop. I wouldn't let you do that to me even when you were human."

Roman pressed himself up by his front paws and met Phil's gaze. *You believe me? You do?*

Phil asked, "What month did we start working together. Make a noise when I say it. January, February, March…"

Roman hit Phil in the chest with his paw and made a yelp noise. *March! March fifteenth we were assigned to the same field office.*

"Hoff," Phil said in defeat. "It's Roman."

Roman jumped off Phil and spun around with his tail high in the air.

"Good job, Roman." Charlie knelt down by him, cuddling and petting him.

I knew it. I knew I could convince him. Roman rubbed his face against Charlie in excitement.

"Everything okay out here, gentlemen?" Vernon walked down the path from the ranch house.

Phil got to his feet, brushing himself off.

When Vernon caught sight of Roman, he panicked. "I'll get the shotgun!"

In unison everyone yelled, "No!"

Roman hid behind Charlie.

Phil approached Vernon. "We have it under control. That's uh…that's one of our trained canine dogs."

"That ain't no dog." Vernon's eyes were wide.

"Yeah. He gets that all the time." Phil gave Roman a quick glance. "He's a wolf-shepherd mix. One of our best. So no need to worry." Phil tried to get Vernon to go back into the house.

Roman walked in front of Nick and sat down, looking at him. *You believe too, Nick?*

"Is it true? Is it really you, Roman?"

Roman used one paw to poke at his leg. *It's me.*

"You men want to head back to the cabin again?" Charlie asked, "Now that you believe us?"

A stabbing pain hit Roman where he sat. The discussion became a ringing in his ears and he fell to his side.

Charlie immediately held him close. "Hang in there, babe. Ride it out."

Roman clenched his teeth and shut his eyes hating this life, the changing sapped all his energy and he was sick of it.

He howled in pain and the sound got stuck in his throat. Shivering and cold, Roman used his nails to claw the ground and pray for it to pass.

When he could breathe again Roman could see his arm around Charlie where he held onto him. "I'm me."

"You are," Charlie said, "Believe us now?"

Nick and Phil hurried to Roman's side. "How can this be possible?" Nick asked.

"I don't know."

Charlie helped Roman to his feet. "He's freezing. I need to get him warm."

"Phil…"

"Yes, Roman." Phil gripped Roman's hand as they made their way back to the cabin.

"The graffiti in that room. The one I was in before this happened…"

"I remember some of it. It was pitch dark in that building."

"Go back and photograph it. Every inch."

Phil took out his phone.

Roman's head began to ache. He spotted the clothing on the floor and slipped the sweatpants on while Charlie helped steady him.

Suzie said, "I'll make a pot of coffee," and headed to the kitchen.

Needing a nap, Roman allowed Charlie to escort him to the couch, sitting with him, holding onto him for comfort. "Thank you, Charlie." He pecked him on the lips.

"You're welcome, Roman." Charlie glanced nervously at the men at their overt sign of attachment.

"They know I'm gay."

Charlie nodded but didn't reply.

Phil flipped his phone closed and said, "The tech boys are on their way. You think the room had something to do with this?" Both Phil and Nick sat on the sofa opposite them.

"Yes. It had to. The last thing I remember was Phil taking the right side of the hall and I was searching the left." Phil nodded in agreement. "I could see some of the paint on the walls with my flashlight, but soon there was a mist or smoke, and my light was ineffective."

Suzie returned with a tray carrying a pot of coffee and mugs, placing it down.

"Thank you, Suzie." Charlie smiled at her.

She nodded and sat on the floor beside them.

"I recall smelling something strong, but I couldn't identify the odor," Phil said as he stirred milk into a mug.

"It nearly knocked me out. I fell to the floor and that's when everything became a blur." Roman rubbed his face tiredly.

Charlie squeezed Roman's hand.

"You fucking vanished, Roman. Completely," Phil said.

"Not completely. I was there watching you guys regroup at the hotel. Remember that crow you all were trying to kill?"

Phil looked defeated. "How the hell were we supposed to know that was you?'

"Because it *was* me. I was doing everything I could to make you guys realize it wasn't a normal crow."

"Calm down." Charlie caressed Roman's hair. "I wonder if strong emotions make the changes come quicker."

That idea made Roman take pause. "You could be right, Charlie."

"Then keep it steady." Charlie rubbed Roman's shoulder.

"It never occurred to me the changes may be linked to my emotions, but that makes perfect sense."

Suzie said, "We looked up the local Indian tribe because at first Roman thought it was a shaman."

Nick shook his head. "There aren't any shamans in this area of America. They're more an Eastern Europe phenomenon. And the medicine people are spiritual healers. I can't imagine them doing this."

Roman thought about a cup of coffee but didn't pour one. He was thirsty, but not for that. He made a move to stand.

"What do you need?" Charlie asked.

"Water."

"I'll get it," Suzie replied.

"Thanks." Roman gathered his thoughts. "There was an inverted pentagram painted on the wall, but it had been obscured so…" Roman felt a wave of something and shook his head. "No."

"Is it coming again?" Charlie wrapped his arm around Roman's shoulder, drawing him closer.

Phil and Nick sat up on the sofa. "Roman? You turning into something?"

Suzie brought a bottle of water for him. Roman poured half on top of his head and drank the other half down.

They all waited.

Roman felt it subside. "Where was I?"

"Inverted pentagram." Phil appeared devastated and Roman had no idea what to say to comfort him.

"Right. So now my thoughts are turning from the Nations to a cult. Witches? Something pagan to do with Mother Nature? I have no idea. But if it was just a simple satanic curse, why the crow and the wolf?'

Charlie dabbed at a drop of water running down Roman's temple.

He connected to Charlie's eyes and immediately felt a carnal craving to make love to him. "Charlie…"

"Yes, Roman?"

"I want to fuck you."

~

Charlie choked and felt his cheeks go crimson.

Suzie giggled.

"Agent Dean," Charlie asked, "Was he like this before the curse?"

Phil smiled wryly. "He never said that to me."

Roman said, "I wanted to fuck you too, Phil, but not as much as Charlie."

Nick waved his hand to interrupt. "When did this become about sex? Roman, tell us more about what happened to you that night."

"He gets this way when he's human because he can manage a quickie." Charlie could sense Roman about to become amorous. "Babe, while you can. Tell them everything."

Roman stuck his hand between Charlie's legs and massaged his balls as he spoke. Charlie tensed up and looked at everyone's reaction.

"I remember a woman's face painted red with white and blue stripes. She was leading some kind of ritual with dancing and singing."

Charlie didn't have his hat nearby so he took one of the throw pillows from where he sat and covered Roman's hand. Suzie gave him a wink and blushed as red as Charlie felt his own cheeks were, while the two agents were attempting to pretend this was all business.

"I was paralyzed, lying on the floor, then suddenly I remember seeing the full moon over me, and I was naked. They danced in a circle around me."

It was as if Charlie could visualize the scene before him.

A ring of fire, chanting echoing in the woods, and Roman lying on his back helpless.

"They spattered blood on me. I could see mostly birds were being held by their feet with their throats cut, but I'm recalling hearts, animal hearts dripping blood as well."

Charlie shut his eyes as Roman massaged his crotch. The dull noise of a beating drum and stomping feet made the hair rise on his skin.

"Then I was surrounded by them, all kneeling around me. They painted me blood-red from the soles of my feet to my hair. Every one of them put their hands between my legs and said something I couldn't understand."

"Can you ID any of them?" Phil asked.

"Only that one woman's face. The red painted one. She was wearing a feather crown and the skin of a wolf on top of her head."

"I could understand how you would assume that would be part of the Indian Nation."

Charlie relaxed his knees wider from the arousing touch. He rested his head on the back of the couch as the chanting grew louder in his ears. A scent of something burning wafted up his nose. Burning bones? Flesh? Herbs?

"I woke naked and crawled to a lake to wash the caked blood off. It wasn't long after that I became a crow and headed back to look for you guys."

Through a haze, Charlie heard Suzie describing the doe that had been found on the west side of their ranch.

The light grew dim and Charlie could see the sky filled with stars through the tips of the tall trees. His cock was thick in his pants and Roman's friction was so exciting he was edging a climax.

"So Charlie and Suzie started researching anything they could find about the legends in this area," Roman said, "Maybe you guys can consult the local sheriff's departments and see if this type of activity has been going on for some time."

Charlie rolled his head on what felt like, dirt, the ground. A red ring of fire surrounded him and he grew cold. It was as if Roman had opened his pants and was holding his naked cock under the blind of the pillow. It made Charlie shiver. He was about to scold his lover for being so bold with people in the room. When he opened his eyes, a woman's red-painted face appeared. He had seen her once before, in the reflection of his bathroom mirror.

Am I imagining this?

She held a bird over his chest, allowing its slit throat to drip blood on his skin.

Charlie shook his head side to side, trying to wake from the odd dream. He glanced down at himself and he was completely naked, blood spattered all over his skin.

"Was anything found at the scene?" Roman asked, "Did you guys end up making any arrests?"

"No," Nick said, "We found nothing. Not a sign of any weapons, chemical storage, gambling, nothing. We were wondering if we either got bad intel or this was a tactic used to divert our attention away from the real location."

Hands were rubbing blood all over Charlie's skin. He tried to move, to get away and run, but he couldn't. His body was paralyzed and he could not shake the sensation of being touched by many in a spot he thought only Roman was touching him in reality. He tried to clear his vision, but it felt as if red smoke was in his eyes.

"I think it was a diversionary tactic. I have no doubt there is a problem in this area, but that information on that particular building was bad info."

Charlie shivered and could not focus on the conversation. Roman's touch between his legs was driving him crazy. But there was no way he was going to climax in front of two ATF agents and Suzie Norman.

He opened his lips to tell Roman to stop, it was too embarrassing. Nothing came out when he tried to speak.

One of the agent's cell phone rang. Phil stood and walked away from the group with the phone to his ear. "Agent Dean…" He cupped it and said, "They photographed the graffiti, Roman."

"Tell them to email it to my mailbox," Nick said, taking out his iPhone.

"This screen is bigger, Nick. Suzie, give me your email address."

Charlie was coated in sweat and writhing on the ground of the forest. He felt slightly sick, but it passed. The chanting grew louder and his legs were parted.

"…at college dot org. Let me log on," Suzie said.

"Yeah, go ahead and send them, we're all waiting."

Charlie threw his head back and gasped. "Roman…"

"Charlie?"

"Not here, Roman. Don't make me come here." Charlie felt so much pleasure between his legs he began riding it, floating above everyone in the room.

"Charlie. Charlie, wake up. Are you all right?"

A slap on his face startled Charlie. He blinked and found everyone staring. Immediately he looked at the pillow on his lap. Roman was kneeling beside the computer, his hand was not where he thought it was. "Did I fall asleep?"

Suzie said, "Your eyes were open."

"Here you go, Roman." Phil moved the laptop to face him. "Is this what you remember?"

Charlie struggled to stand, putting the pillow on the couch and staggering to the bathroom to splash his face.

"Babe?" Roman appeared concerned.

"Just need to wake up. Sorry." Charlie closed the bathroom door and rinsed his hands and face. He opened his pants to pee and jumped at the sight of a reddish color smeared on his cock. In terror he dragged his jeans down his legs and felt faint.

~

Roman heard Charlie make a noise of fear or shock. "Hang on." He held up one finger and walked to the bathroom, opening the door. "What's wrong, Charlie?"

"What the hell?" Charlie gestured to his crotch. "Were you touchin' me?"

"When?" Roman got to his knees and tugged Charlie's pants and briefs down. "Where are you cut?"

"I have to sit. I feel like I'm about to pass out."

Roman tugged Charlie's boots off, then his pants and briefs. He used a wet washcloth to remove the blood. "There's nothing here."

"Roman?" Phil spoke from outside the door. "Our forensic guy just matched the symbols to a coven that's been making animal sacrifices in the Deer Creek reservoir area."

"Okay, Phil." Roman lowered his voice. "There's no cut, Charlie. You're not bleeding."

Charlie couldn't catch his breath. "Roman, I must have fell asleep 'cause I had a dream out there on the couch."

"You okay in there, guys?"

"Be right out." Roman met Charlie's eyes. "What was it about?"

"The thing that happened to you..." Charlie looked down at his crotch. Roman had washed all the reddish color from him. He tugged on his cock, checking it out for himself. "I was lying on the ground looking at the stars."

The expression on Roman's face became grim.

"Just like what you described." Charlie held onto his balls, cupping them. "But it was just me thinkin' of what you was sayin', right?"

"If it was just you thinking it, how would you get blood on your dick?"

"What's that supposed to mean?" Charlie gripped Roman's arm and squeezed.

"I don't know. I wish I did, Charlie, but nothing is making sense to me anymore." Roman stood. "You feel okay enough to join us? I think Phil has figured out some possible suspects."

Staring at Roman, and even more interestingly, smelling him, made Charlie crave him. Charlie ran his tongue over his teeth inside his mouth in hunger. A powerful urge to dominate Roman seized Charlie. He attacked Roman, pushing him against the wall and went for his mouth. Roman reacted, digging one hand into Charlie's hair and gripping his entire package in the other.

Feeling like an unleashed animal, Charlie sucked on Roman's tongue and began undressing him, tugging the shirt over his head.

Roman brought them both to the floor, lips locked together.

Charlie toppled Roman over in the small space between the tub and the door. He worked Roman's sweatpants off and began poking his stiff cock between Roman's legs.

"Let me in, you motherfucker." Charlie snarled, showing his teeth, feeling extremely aggressive.

In response, Roman submitted, spreading his legs and opening himself up.

Charlie tried to penetrate Roman but grew frustrated when he couldn't. He stood, opened the medicine chest and grabbed petroleum jelly. Taking two fingers he scooped some out and knelt back on the floor. Roman made a move under him.

Charlie didn't know if it was to get up or not. He growled. "You ain't goin' nowhere." He used his two coated fingers to push his way inside Roman's back passage.

Roman moaned and closed his eyes.

"Guys?" Phil's voice spoke from outside the door.

Of Wolves and Men

"Leave us a minute!" Charlie met Roman's eyes and loved the gleam in them. "You're mine. You got that?" He placed one hand on either side of Roman's body while Roman held his own knees, exposing himself.

"I got it."

Charlie pointed his cock at Roman's rim and pushed through the thick gel. Deeper and deeper, Charlie felt Roman's muscles clench and then release under him. The impulse to come was overwhelming. Yes, Charlie loved sex, but this drive was beyond his wildest dreams.

The raw scent of Roman's sexuality made Charlie crazy. He knelt upright, held Roman's thighs and began humping him. Suddenly the small room was echoing with snarls and growls of passion. Charlie stared at Roman's cock as it grew semi-erect, and then stiff. As he fucked, he inhaled Roman's scent like he'd never smelled another aroma so intriguing. Getting closer to a climax, Charlie cupped Roman's chest, hammering inside him as Roman showed his teeth in a sensual snarl. The friction and smells made Charlie rise to a climax quickly. When Roman gripped the back of his head and met his mouth, Charlie came. He pushed as hard as he could, connecting them on the deepest level. Roman whimpered in Charlie's mouth in complete surrender.

Coated in sweat, Charlie pulled out, dropping between Roman's legs to suck his cock. Roman held onto his inner thighs, surrounding Charlie's hands, which gripped the base of his dick.

Charlie drew long suction to the tip and felt like howling he was so high. Roman's cock pulsated strongly, indicating he was about to come. Charlie increased the pace and tasted Roman's spunk. With it pooled on his tongue, Charlie sat upright, tilted back his head and let it slide down his throat like an oyster. Roman rubbed his face all over Charlie's chest and neck, sniffing, licking him and letting out tiny noises of pleasure.

Charlie reciprocated, rubbing his body and cheek all over Roman to exchange their scents.

They lay panting, on the bathroom throw rug, trying to recuperate. "I have never felt this way about no one, in my life." Charlie knew he could sleep where he was, on top of Roman.

"Never." Roman held him closer.

"Look, guys," Phil tapped the door as he said, "I know there's a time and place for everything, but…we may have a lead here. And we can use your help, Roman."

"Babe." Roman touched Charlie gently. "I don't know how much longer I'll be me."

Charlie seemed to come aware. He shook his head to clear his brain and allowed Roman to move. "I don't know what come over me, Roman. I'm sorry."

Roman began washing up at the sink. "Don't be. It was wonderful."

Charlie felt slightly embarrassed. He waited his turn at the sink, wondering why he behaved so badly.

Beside him, Roman put his sweatpants and t-shirt back on. "You okay?"

"Huh? Yeah. Go on. I'll be there in a minute."

Roman gave him a kiss and left the bathroom.

Charlie dressed and tried to think about what he had done. Something had changed in him. He would never behave like that before. Not with three people in the living room waiting for them. He looked into the mirror and asked himself, "What's got into you, Mosby?"

Chapter 12

Roman exited the bathroom expecting the change. A strong climax, growing angry, frustration, all seemed to trigger it. It was something he didn't consider before, but it was dead on. He had learned meditation and self control, in both his professional and private life. It was time he considered a method for bringing this chaos under control.

"Roman, come here." Phil and Nick were sitting on the sofa in front of the computer. "The local sheriff's department reported dozens of animals killed the same way as the doe. The hearts have all been cut out."

Nick said, "And there have been missing persons' reports as well. A cluster right in the same ten mile radius as the raid we did last week."

"Is Charlie okay?" Suzie asked.

Roman glanced back at the bathroom door. "Yeah. I think he's just tired."

"Looks like you guys may be here for a while. Do you want me to ask Mom and Sherlane to cook you up something to eat?"

"I wouldn't mind." Nick shrugged. "If it isn't imposing, Suzie."

"Not at all." She smiled and left the cabin.

"Nice girl."

"She's single. Go get her, Phil." Roman smiled.

"I wouldn't mind asking her out."

Roman's attention moved to the bathroom door. Charlie exited, looking run down and weary. He reached out his hand. Charlie took it, sitting on the floor beside him.

"Right." Nick scrolled through pages of reports. "This is photographs of other suspected tags from the same coven."

Roman leaned close to the laptop. "That's it. I recognize the symbols." He heard Charlie sniffing him. Roman glanced at him. Charlie had his nose in Roman's shirt.

"There's an FBI file on this group." Nick tapped more keys. "I can do more from our office tomorrow. Will you survive 'til then, Roman?"

"If I don't get caught up in a leg trap." He felt Charlie rubbing his cheek against him and wondered if he was just very tired.

"Stay inside here. In the cabin."

Phil rose up. "I guess we're going to miss that free meal."

"Go on up to the ranch house. Vernon wouldn't mind." Roman pointed in the direction. "Sherlane is the brunette. She's Vernon's oldest daughter. It's time you settled down, Phil. And you too, Nick. Both of you are single."

"We're too busy," Nick replied, "and we travel constantly. I don't have to tell you that."

"I know." Roman asked Charlie, "You feeling okay?"

"Huh?" Charlie's blue eyes appeared hazy, as if he were overtired.

"Go to bed, babe."

Charlie didn't answer. He leaned back against the foot of the sofa, staring into space.

Roman walked the two agents to the door. "Seriously, go eat. The family is very nice."

"Sure, why not." Nick stared at Roman. "I'm glad we found you, Burk. The place isn't the same without you."

"I'm glad you found me too."

"Get back to your desk, will ya?"

"Sure. I'll probably be a crow and shit on all your paperwork." Roman smiled at Phil. "I'll talk to you soon. And if I can't, Charlie will."

Phil said, "We'll have the answer to this soon, Roman. I promise."

Roman wished he could believe that. He closed the door and glanced back at Charlie. "I think this is the longest I've gone without a change."

"Huh?"

"You okay, Charlie?" Roman sat next to him.

Charlie stuck his nose into Roman's shirt and sniffed.

It would amuse Roman if it weren't for the implications. Roman wrapped his arm around Charlie's shoulder and held him against his chest.

Chapter 13

Charlie woke in the night. He ran his hand over the bed beside him. An owl hooted outside the window and the strong wind battered the branches of a paper birch against the glass. The bathroom door opened and the inside light shut off. A shadowy silhouette moved across the floor. Roman crawled back into bed.

"How come you're still a man?" Charlie reached out to touch his cheek.

"I have no idea other than keeping my temper and emotions under control. You were right. Anger is a particularly quick trigger."

"Do you think Phil and Nick will find a way to release you from the curse?'

Roman sealed their bodies together under the blankets. "I hope so. I figure they're on the right track. The symbols they located fit the ones in the room I entered, where I got sick."

"I like you here in my bed." Charlie slid his arm under Roman and curled him into an embrace. "You smell so good. I don't know what it is about your scent." He inhaled Roman's neck. "Makes my dick thick."

Roman chuckled softly, caressing Charlie's hair.

"If they can get rid of this curse, I assume you'll go back to work. Right?" Charlie rested his leg over Roman's thigh.

"Yes. I would."

"And…your office is in Reno, so…"

"I'd still see you, when I could."

A sinking sensation filled Charlie's gut. "Is it selfish for me to want you to stay as you are?"

"Yes. But I get it."

Charlie leaned back to stare into Roman's eyes. "I feel like I don't know anything about you."

"We haven't had much time to talk. Most of the time I'm howling or cawing."

"It's like there's a fuse lit and I have to hurry up or you'll vanish."

"I don't know what to say to that, Charlie. If I can be rid of this curse, would you move to Reno?"

"And? Do what?"

"I don't know. Be a rodeo cowboy?" Roman's eyes twinkled in the dimness.

"Ha. Ha."

"Let's take it a day at a time. We don't know what will happen tomorrow. And even if Phil and Nick figure out who has done this to me, they still have to find them and make them take the curse off."

"And that could take months, right?"

"God, I hope not."

Charlie tried not to take the comment as an insult. He knew how painful the change was and he didn't want Roman to suffer either. But he'd miss him once he was gone.

Charlie pressed Roman back against the pillows and kissed him, resting his body on top of Roman's, using his knees to spread Roman's legs.

Roman opened himself up for the taking.

Smoothing his hand down Roman's side to his hip, Charlie swirled his tongue in his mouth, moaning as the fire was lit between them. He squeezed the powerful muscle on Roman's leg, loving his size and strength. Charlie leaned on his elbow and ground his cock against Roman's. When he made a growling noise, both he and Roman paused in their kiss.

"Was that me?"

"Wasn't me," Roman replied.

"You must be rubbing off on me."

"I'm 'rubbing off' right now." Roman created hot friction by humping Charlie. "Get the petroleum jelly."

Charlie pecked Roman's lips and hopped off the bed. He jogged to the bathroom, returning quickly. Roman's eyes were glowing in the dark, green, like traffic signals. He was holding his cock, stroking it, keeping it hard.

"You still with me, Roman?" Charlie crawled back to his original place, kneeling over Roman's body.

"Still me." He scooted lower on the bed and held onto his knees, pulling his legs wide apart.

Hoping the sex would not create a wolf in his bed, Charlie repeated what he had done earlier in the bathroom, using the thick gel up Roman's ass.

Roman hissed, like he was sucking air between clenched teeth.

Charlie proceeded with caution. Roman hadn't changed earlier when they had sex. He was hoping he didn't this time either.

Pointing his cock downwards, aiming at that inviting puckered rim, Charlie pushed inside Roman and felt every fiber in his body shiver. "I do love making love to you, Roman."

"Same here, Charlie."

Propped up on his hands, Charlie inched closer, penetrating as deeply as he could. The scent of Roman's crotch was making Charlie insane. He inhaled that tantalizing aroma and began a rhythm of thrusting, slowly at first, but as deep as he could go inside his man.

Roman relaxed under him, touching his own cock to keep it interested. The sight of everything Roman did and the expression of lust on his face, put Charlie near the edge quickly.

"I want to hump you like a hound dog."

"I'm not stopping you."

Taking another sniff of the air, Charlie braced himself and began hammering into his lover. As he grunted and groaned, he growled as well. The pleasure made Charlie show his teeth in a sensual snarl. As the impulse to come became a tide he couldn't hold back, Charlie jerked his hips against Roman and howled in delight.

A faint echo of a coyote returning the call was carried on the wind.

Sweat pouring out of Charlie's skin, he pulled out and dropped down on Roman so he could suck his cock, both hands holding the base.

Roman began riding the friction, his hips rising off the bed. Huffing noises, deep guttural growls and snarls followed.

Charlie didn't care. He wanted his wolf—his man, his beast—to climax.

Roman's length pulsated in Charlie's mouth. The load of cum tasted divine. He swallowed it down and sucked until nothing more came out of Roman's slit.

While Roman recuperated, Charlie lapped up and down his cock, going mad for the aroma and taste. He didn't want to stop, but they were both exhausted and spent.

He crawled up the bed to drop down beside Roman. Roman's eyes were closed and he drifted off to sleep. Charlie cradled him in his arms and felt as possessive as a mother with her youngster. He rocked Roman against him, pressing his lips to his neck so he could taste him.

~

Morning came and Charlie awoke. He never used a clock to get up in the morning. The minute six a.m. hit, he was awake. As he climbed out of bed, he was stunned to see Roman still in human form, asleep beside him.

"Son of a bitch. Is he cured?" Charlie didn't question fate. He had no control over it.

Once in the shower, he noticed the door opening. When he peeked out, he found Roman relieving himself in the toilet.

"Sorry I woke you."

"No problem." Roman climbed into the shower with him.

Charlie laughed. "Never did a tandem shower before. It's kinda cozy."

"Kind of erotic you mean." Roman soaped up Charlie's genitals.

"Why are you still a man? You had all sorts of trouble controlling it until last night."

"I'm not sure, Charlie. I'm praying whatever it was had a time limit, and I'm done. But I've been trying to keep my mind free of anger and strong bad emotions."

Charlie relinquished the spray to Roman so he could wash. "That may be it. I mean, I keep expectin' you to be somethin' else if I blink. But to have you in my bed overnight?" Charlie whistled. "That was a treat."

"I agree." Roman grabbed at Charlie's cock playfully.

Their laughter echoed in the wet room. "You'll get me late. I usually am up at the house five minutes out of my bed."

"So it'll be ten." Roman connected them at the groin, holding both their cocks upright together.

"I'm an insatiable animal with you." Charlie shivered and braced himself on the walls.

"I know. Me too. I can't get enough of our sex." Roman used both his hands to jack them off.

"If you keep that up, it won't take five minutes." Charlie stared down at the action. "I never seen anythin' like it."

"I'm about to blow…" Roman fisted them in a blur of motion.

Charlie heard him howl and couldn't stop himself from joining in. As the climax hit, he grabbed Roman's jaw and sucked at his lips and tongue. Squeaking noises came from

Of Wolves and Men

Roman, little canine whimpers. Charlie backed up and asked, "You turnin'?"

"Huh?" Roman appeared slightly dazed. "Fuck that felt good."

Charlie waited. Roman spun around and rinsed off under the spray. "I'm starving. What do they usually cook up at the ranch house?" He shut the taps and grabbed two towels, handing Charlie one.

"Good grub. All of it."

"Can't wait." Roman grinned at him and threw the towel over the rack.

~

Harley started barking like mad as Charlie opened the door to the ranch house. The dog snapped at Roman's legs, going crazy.

"Dog, you are a pain in the butt!" Charlie picked him up and tossed him outside, shutting the door quickly. Harley continued to bark loudly.

"He don't like you."

"I don't like him either." Roman shook his head.

When Roman and Charlie entered the kitchen, Connie was busy at the stove while Sherlane and Suzie picked up empty plates. Roman met Suzie's eyes. She smiled. "Hungry?"

"Starved."

"Have a seat."

Charlie took off his hat and joined him. "Did we miss the boys?"

"Yeah, they were here and gone." Sherlane poured both Charlie and Roman coffee.

"Thank you." Roman raised his cup in greeting. "I'm Roman."

"I know who you are." Sherlane grinned slyly. "Everyone does now."

"Oh?" Roman glanced at Charlie. He wasn't sure how to interpret that.

"Here ya go, boys." Connie set two helpings of flapjacks, bacon, and sausage in front of them. "Biscuits and gravy too."

"Wow." Roman began eating, taking huge bites.

"Thank you, Connie," Charlie said.

"My pleasure, Charlie. There's plenty more."

"This is superb." Roman felt as if he hadn't had a proper meal at a table in ages.

Suzie sat with them. "You…um…okay now?"

"I don't know." Roman wiped his mouth on a napkin. "I was me all night."

"Maybe it's gone?" She tilted her head.

"I doubt it. But I hope so."

"How you doin', Charlie?" she asked.

He nodded, mouth full, eating quickly. "Late."

"Those fellas from the ATF were sure nice." Sherlane stood behind Charlie, putting her hand on his shoulder. "I liked that Phil fella."

"He's a good guy." Roman sipped his coffee. "He could use a nice woman to keep him in line."

"All you men can." Connie held the coffee pot over Charlie's cup, topping him off.

"True." Sherlane giggled.

"Not all." Roman glanced at Charlie and winked.

Charlie blushed and scooped more food into his mouth. "How much of a head start did those boys get?"

"You mean, Butch, JP, and Goat?" Suzie looked at the clock. "Not long. Fifteen minutes?"

"Shoot." Charlie ate another bite of food. "I have to head up to the barn, Roman. You sit and finish."

"I can help you."

"Uh, them horses aren't happy about you hangin' 'round them. You just eat and chat with the women."

Of Wolves and Men

"Charlie," Roman said, knowing he didn't want to become a wolf in the kitchen. "I'll come."

As if he finally got the message, Charlie nodded. He stood and brought his plate to the sink, handing it to Connie. "Wonderful as usual. Thanks, Connie."

"You're very welcome, Charlie."

Roman finished the food on his plate and did the same. "I could eat a few helpings of that, easy."

"Anytime. No one goes hungry here."

Charlie grabbed his coat and made for the door. Roman was wearing one of his old ones. The minute they opened the door, Harley was there waiting, ready to bark and bite. Charlie nudged him inside and again put a door between them.

They jogged to the barn. Roman knew Charlie had a job to do, and he hoped to help him out. A truck load of workers had arrived and were busy inside the barn cleaning stalls and grooming the horses.

Charlie headed for the open barn doors. Instantly, the sound of the horses making noises of distress became loud. Roman stopped in his tracks. "Shit."

"I figured. Stay out here."

"Tell me what I can do to help?"

"Don't scare the ponies." Charlie laughed and entered the barn.

Roman backed up, knowing his scent was as terrifying to the horses as his presence. He stuffed his hands into the jacket pockets and looked out at the horizon. A rider was coming down the mountain path. Roman made out the patches on the painted horse before he could see who was riding it. Butch. It was Butch coming down the hillside.

As Butch drew near, Roman spotted something hanging from the saddle. The rage in his blood was instant. He raced towards Butch to confront him.

Butch's horse reared and showed the whites of its eyes in panic at Roman's approach.

Butch tried to control him, as he suddenly turned into a bucking bronco rider. "You're scaring my horse! What the hell's the matter with you? Easy, Scout, easy boy."

"What did you do to her!" Roman clenched his teeth.

"To her? Are you referring to my gelding?" Butch hopped off his horse, gripping onto the rein to prevent the horse from fleeing. "It's a he without balls, Roman, not a 'her'."

Roman pointed to the dead coyote lying upside down on the horse's back. "You killed her?"

Charlie must have heard the commotion because he hurried towards them.

Roman grabbed the dead coyote and wailed as he recognized her as the she-coyote that had followed him to the ranch. "Why? What did she do to you?"

"I didn't kill her!" Butch struggled to keep Scout under control. "And if I did? They're considered a nuisance and we can kill as many as we like."

Roman attacked Butch. The horse reared and bucked as several men tried to contain it.

~

Charlie raced to the scene of the battle in fear. The minute Roman dove at Butch, he changed. An enormous black wolf was on top of Butch, trying to rip his throat out.

The clothing fell off of Roman as Charlie wrapped both arms around him from behind, trying to pull him off. Roman spun back and bit Charlie's hand.

Charlie reacted in pain, but didn't let go. "Roman! Calm down!"

"What the hell?" Butch wrestled with the big wolf. "I can't believe my eyes! This is Roman? He was just a man! Charlie, get him off me! I didn't kill the coyote. Her heart was cut out!"

Of Wolves and Men

"Roman! Are you listening? She was killed by the cult. Calm down!" The spot where Charlie was bitten began to bleed and throb painfully.

A distinct sound of a shotgun chambering a round made Charlie turn to look. Vernon had his gun pointed at Roman, his finger on the trigger.

"No! Vernon! That's Roman! Don't you dare shoot!"

"I don't care who the hell it is. If he don't stop attacking Butch, he's dead!"

Charlie strengthened his hold on Roman and roared as he picked the big wolf up, off of Butch. Butch scrambled to his feet, gasping for breath.

Roman went limp in his arms, whimpering the saddest sound Charlie had ever heard. He forced Roman to the ground and knelt on him, pinning him. "He didn't kill her. Are you hearin' me?"

Roman lay still under Charlie, his gaze in the direction of the dead animal.

"Put that gun away." Charlie caught his breath.

Vernon lowered the barrel. "What did I just see, Charlie? You got some explaining to do."

"It's a curse." Charlie lessened his hold on Roman, but didn't let go. "Poor Roman's under a spell. Don't you believe he wants to be this way for a minute."

"If I didn't see it with my own eyes." Butch untied the coyote from the saddle and laid her down beside Roman. "Look. You can see the same thing that happened to that doe happened to her. Honest. I didn't do nothing but bring her back for Doc McMurray to see."

Roman closed his eyes and used his paw to cover them.

If Charlie thought wolves couldn't weep, he was wrong. The emotional pain Roman was enduring was extreme.

As Roman calmed down, Charlie looked at his hand. Roman's sharp teeth had cut him down to the bone. He shook his arm to rid the pain but he needed to stop the bleeding.

While Roman stayed still against the cold ground, Charlie felt him change again. He slid off Roman, resting his hand on his back. "Get me them clothes, Butch."

"I'm not going near him."

"Goat, can you?" Charlie reached out to the pile.

Goat crept over to the clothing, looking terrified.

Roman groaned in agony and slowly became a man while everyone watched in awe.

"Thank you, Goat."

"We need a priest. Someone has to perform an exorcism or something." Goat backed up once he dropped Roman's clothing next to him.

"Maybe. Go call the local minister, Goat. I'm willing to try anything." Roman was shivering as Charlie helped him get dressed. Slowly Roman sat up, sliding on the jeans and putting the t-shirt over his head.

Charlie looked around at the group of working men, gaping at him. "Butch, get these wranglers back to work. The barn won't clean itself." He checked his hand and was upset with how bad the bite was.

"Okay, boys. Show's over." Vernon waved them back into the barn.

Roman put the jacket on then inspected the coyote. "Baby. What did they do to you?" He petted her coat gently.

"Did you know this animal?" Charlie asked. "Was she one of you?"

"No. She wasn't. We just met one night. She was very sweet."

"I'm sorry, Roman." Charlie stood up stiffly. "I need a first aid kit. You gave me a good bite."

"No!" Roman hopped to his feet and grabbed Charlie's hand. "I'm so sorry. I didn't know I did it."

"I know." Charlie rubbed his back. "Vernon, can you call the sheriff's office and tell them about the latest sacrifice? Me and Roman will call the ATF agents."

"I should tell the sheriff about Roman." Vernon walked back to the house, shaking his head, the shotgun still in his hand. "Too many crazy things going on lately."

"I'm sorry, Vernon!" Roman called after him, then bit his lip and looked at Charlie.

The tears in Roman's eyes broke Charlie's heart. "Here. Call Phil." Charlie handed him his phone and entered the barn to wrap his hand up.

JP helped him. "You should go to the emergency room, Charlie. You need stitches."

"I'm okay." He knew he wasn't. He used disinfectant spray and the sting nearly made him scream. JP wrapped gauze around his hand to stop the bleeding.

~

"Phil? Roman. Look, the cult just sacrificed a coyote at the ranch."

"Shit. We have every agency in the area a BOLO alert, Roman. We will find them."

"Well, get our group up here and let's comb the area by the reservoir. That's where all these animals are being dumped." Roman made a move towards the barn to see how Charlie was. The horses were in the open paddock so it was empty. When he stood at the open barn door, the workers gave him a look like he was Satan. Many made the sign of the cross and backed away from him.

"Okay. I'll get the troops together. What's the best access to that area?"

Roman left the barn and knew Vernon would not be happy with his tourist trade being infiltrated with federal and state officials. "I have a feeling the best way up to that area is through this ranch, but Mr. Norman will not be pleased."

"I'll check the topography and see if there's a back road in. You said by the reservoir?"

"Yes. The area I suspect is the border between this ranch and the federal reserve." He noticed Charlie coming out of the barn, gauze wrapped around his hand. It was obviously painful since Charlie was still nursing it, holding his hand upwards.

"Okay, Roman. I'll get back to you when we have everything organized."

Roman flipped the phone shut and handed it to Charlie. "Phil's getting a group together to search up by the west fence." He moved closer. "You okay? How badly did I get you?"

"Bad. I'm wondering whether to go to the hospital for a stitch."

"No. Oh, Christ. I'm so sorry."

"Ya fight a wolf, ya get bit."

"Look, Charlie..." Roman held his injured hand gently. "My influence here has been devastating to you. As if the mess I've made of your job isn't bad enough. Now I've bitten you."

"Don't fret. Okay?"

Roman glanced at the hive of activity that surrounded them. The wranglers were busy cleaning and tending sixty horses. "Does Vernon have a tourist ride up to the mountains scheduled?"

"I assume so."

"Yeah. About that." Roman rubbed his face tiredly. "This place is going to be a swarm of government agents within an hour. I need to tell him."

Charlie appeared grim. "I think Vernon is already at the end of his rope with this."

"I know. Hopefully the agents will find these morons, arrest them, and I can get on with my life." The minute he said it, he could see the effect on Charlie's face.

"Yeah, you do that, Roman. You go ahead and get on with your life. I need to do the same thing."

"Charlie…" Roman called after him as he walked away. He looked at the sun coming up over the horizon and sighed.

G. A. Hauser

Chapter 14

Charlie tried to continue working but blood kept seeping through his bandages. He saddled Spirit and walked out of the barn staring at the morning sunlight sparkling on the frosted ground.

Most of the wranglers were finished cleaning the barn and were spreading hay in the open paddock for the horses to graze on. Charlie heard Vernon raising his voice and looked down the drive. He and Roman were in a heated debate.

Charlie exhaled a vaporous breath in the chilled air and nudged Spirit to walk towards the two men. Before Charlie had closed the gap between them, a caravan of black SUVs and sedans, marked patrol units from Utah State Patrol, the local sheriff's departments, as well as a helicopter had arrived.

"Vernon, you are not goin' to be happy with me, are you?" Charlie stopped Spirit and watched the action. Several men in black jackets with white lettering—'FBI', 'ATF', and 'USP'—were exiting their vehicles to talk to Vernon.

He couldn't hear their conversation, but the body language was enough to figure it out. Vernon waved his hands in frustration while the other men obviously were trying to convince him how necessary the search of the area was.

The moment before Charlie turned Spirit away from the group, he met Roman's eyes. The sadness in them was too much for Charlie to bear. *Yes, Roman. You want to get back to your job. Your life. I understand. Who wouldn't?*

Of Wolves and Men

Charlie headed to the west fence line to see if it needed any repairs. Usually with the death of an animal, the fence was damaged.

He heard the clop of hooves on frozen ground and saw Butch riding Scout beside him.

"Your hand still bleeding?" Butch asked.

Charlie didn't answer, assuming JP had filled Butch in on the damage.

"You need to stay away from that guy, Charlie. He's dangerous."

"You mind your own business."

They continued in silence for a while, then Butch offered, "I found the coyote in the exact spot we found the doe."

"Okay." Charlie glanced down at his hand. He was resting it on his lap as he rode. The sting and throb from it was getting worse.

"Are those agents going to search the woods?"

"Yup."

Just as he said it, the helicopter passed overhead.

Spirit snorted and his ears flipped around at the sound.

"We have a group of fifteen trail riders scheduled for noon." Butch shielded his eyes to stare up at the helicopter.

"Great." Charlie had no idea how long it would take the agents to scour the countryside. It was just past seven now.

"Vernon won't take kindly to his business being affected."

"I know!" Charlie was losing his patience. With the anger he felt a twinge of pain in his gut. After a few deep breaths he calmed down and the twisting inside him stopped. Before they arrived at the west fence line, the noise of four-wheel-drive vehicles coming up the trail behind them echoed in the vast space. Charlie stopped Spirit and turned him around while Butch did the same.

"Here they come." Butch shook his head sadly.

"Look, Butch, they got to find this group of sadists. You know? We don't want no more harm comin' to anymore animals or the ponies. Do we?"

"Nope. Better get off the tail before we get run down."

Charlie walked off the dirt path with Butch, stopping to watch the heavy vehicles power up the small bridle trail.

As they passed, Spirit jerked his head up and down in annoyance. Charlie tried to see which car held his man. Now that Roman had figured out how to control the change, he assumed he would head back to Reno. Would he say goodbye? Or just vanish?

A black SUV stopped. Roman got out of the passenger side and Charlie could see Phil driving.

Spirit immediately had a fit at Roman's approach. Charlie controlled the horse, hearing Scout stomping and fussing beside him.

Roman stopped his progress towards the horses. "Charlie."

"Go on. I get it." Charlie nodded to the car idling behind Roman.

Roman hit his hand twice on the roof of the car and Phil continued on. "Butch? Can you head up the mountain and show the boys where you found the coyote?"

"Sure." Butch used his heels to urge Scout on, and Scout seemed more than happy to get away from Roman.

Charlie struggled to keep Spirit under control with one hand. "Come on, boy. Work with me here," Charlie said to the horse.

Roman backed up, obviously trying to keep the horse from growing too nervous.

"I give up." Charlie hopped off of Spirit and took the reins over his neck to hold. He dragged Spirit towards Roman and stood in front of him. "You're leaving. I know."

"No. I'm not going anywhere until this is resolved. These people who did this to me are here. Not in Reno."

"Right. So you're staying back just for that. Okay." Charlie felt his heart break.

"Charlie..." Roman reached for him.

Charlie backed away. Spirit stomped, the whites of his eyes showing. Charlie's hand began stinging and more blood seeped through the bandages.

"You should have gone to the hospital, Charlie." Roman tilted his head to his hand. "It's still bleeding."

"Why don't you stop telling me what to do?" Charlie watched the last vehicle in the caravan vanish behind a stand of evergreens. The helicopter was over the reservoir, making oblong circles in the sky.

"Babe."

"Go. Get lost. You wanted me for the help. Now you got plenty of it." Spirit became increasingly agitated.

"You think I don't care about you?"

"I think you're a selfish bastard. That's what I think." Charlie nearly got toppled over by Spirit. "What is your problem, boy?" He jerked the horse's bridle but the more annoyed Charlie became, the crazier Spirit's behavior was. Trying to control a large gelding male with one hand was not easy. "Look what your being here does to a horse, Roman. If he can't stand you, how am I supposed to feel?"

"Don't say that." Roman glanced over his shoulder, as if checking to see if anyone was still lingering. All the agents and officers were far away by now. "Charlie, I can't help what happened to me. I can't change anything."

"But you will." Charlie's shoulder was jerked as Spirit reared. "God damn it!" He faced the horse and shouted, "Cut it out!"

Spirit went wild, rearing up and kicking out his front legs. Charlie suddenly realized the horse wasn't afraid of Roman, it was afraid of him. "What is with you, Spirit?" He dodged a flailing hoof and the reins were tugged out of his hand. Spirit galloped back to the barn as if he had a demon chasing at his heels. With his mouth gaping in shock, Charlie stood staring after his beloved horse.

He spun around and pointed to Roman. "This is all your fault! I wish you'd never come here. You know that? You have been nothin' but trouble to me from day one."

"I'm sorry. But I needed you. Charlie, you know what I'm up against."

"You? It's always about you!" Charlie's hand burned and throbbed. He pointed at Roman with his good hand. "You have any idea what influence you've had on my life? My job? My emotions? I'm a wreck at the moment. You even think about that?" He swore under his breath and stuck his hand under Roman's nose. "And this? You fuckin' bit me!"

"I didn't mean any of it." Roman wrung his hands in frustration. "I didn't purposely screw you up. You wanted to make love to me as well. Don't act like I was alone in this relationship. You fucked me, didn't you? So don't pretend you got nothing out of this deal."

"A fuck?" Charlie started breathing fire he was so enraged. It felt like a ball of acid began to burn in his belly. "I wasn't even sure I wanted to be gay. I had one blowjob from one fella and you came along and—"

"And?" Roman's eyes widened as his frustration turned to rage. "You wanted me. Don't even pretend this was me pushing you, making you do things you didn't want to do."

"But you did. I didn't know what I wanted. You come along and well…look at the wreck you made of my life."

"Your life?" Roman choked. "You call me a selfish bastard? How would you like to be cursed? What did I do to deserve that? I walked into a room and bang. I'm a fucking wolf or a crow. Don't even try to make me feel sorry for you."

Of Wolves and Men

Charlie puffed up his chest and poked his finger into Roman's. "Fuck you! You got that? Why don't you go back to Reno and bite yourself?"

Roman snarled and pushed Charlie.

Charlie reacted and attacked Roman. They struggled with each other, trying to throw the other one off balance, or topple backwards.

A searing pain hit Charlie. He cringed and closed his eyes. Roman's masculine snarls became rabid and canine. Charlie opened his eyes and the two of them dropped to the hard ground, rolling to gain dominance. Roman's sharp white canines snapped at Charlie. He snapped back and when he tried to yell obscenities, he snarled instead. As they fought, they left a trail of clothing behind. Charlie bit Roman's snout and he bit back.

When Charlie spotted beige fur in Roman's teeth he realized he wasn't a man any longer. Charlie had changed.

On all fours, the two of them fought for dominance. There could only be one alpha male.

Roman rolled to his back, his lips curled to show off his fangs. Both of Roman's front paws were pushing Charlie's chest.

Charlie stood over him, snarling and licking his teeth and nose. *"I'm a fucking wolf! Now look what you did!"*

"I didn't do it! How the hell could I do it?"

"You bit me!"

"That can't be why!"

Charlie straddled Roman's body, staring down at him. *"You son of a bitch. I should kill you!"* He snapped at Roman's neck.

"Don't blame me! I don't have the power to change someone into this!" Roman snapped back, nipping Charlie's snout.

"What am I supposed to do now?"

"How the hell should I know? You think I've figured this mess out?"

Charlie took a look out into the distance. He couldn't believe how far he could see. Sniffing the air, he was hit with so many different scents, he was overwhelmed.

"So? How do you like it?" Roman pushed his big front paw into Charlie's chest.

"I don't know. I can't believe this isn't a weird dream." He heard the helicopter off in the distance, and if he focused, he could hear men's voices. And they had to be nearly three or four miles away.

"I had a feeling when you went into a trance last evening, and there was blood on you…well…"

Charlie looked down at Roman's dark coat, then his beige one. He could only see his front legs. *"You think it's what happened that night? Why didn't I change then?"*

"You didn't get mad."

"I'm not sure I hate this." Charlie sniffed at Roman's fur.

"Are you kidding me? You want to be an animal?" Roman pushed his paw into Charlie's nose.

Charlie nipped at him playfully.

Roman scrambled to his feet and began roughhousing, trying to push Charlie over. Charlie danced around excitedly, his tail high up in the air.

The sense of power and freedom Charlie felt was exhilarating. Leaping and using his snout, he pinned Roman under him again. Roman licked at his mouth and chin in submission. Charlie stood over Roman, one paw on his chest, the other beside him. The cut on his hand was gone.

Charlie sat on his hindquarters and kept looking around. *"Everything is sharp. I can see and hear so many things."*

"I never stopped to enjoy it. I was consumed with fear."

"I understand that." Charlie licked at his nose in affection. *"I just wish we could change at will. You know? I mean, I can't do my job this way. But wouldn't it be fun to spend a few hours a day racing around the hillside?"*

The mobile phone in Charlie's coat pocket rang.

They both perked up and looked.

"*That's either Vernon for me, or Phil for you.*" Charlie walked to where their clothing was and sniffed.

"*We could be a help to Phil. Think about using our senses to find these morons who did this.*"

Charlie wasn't so sure he wanted to. The phone stopped ringing and he nudged the jacket with his paw, but there wasn't much he could do with it.

"*Let's at least head over there.*" Roman stuck his cold, wet nose into Charlie ear.

Charlie shook his head at the tickle. "*What if they don't know it's us and shoot us?*"

"*Phil will know.*"

"*He knows about you. He won't expect two wolves. No way, Roman.*"

"*Come on.*" Roman pranced a few paces in front of him. "*Race me.*"

"*And what if we both turn and are naked and our clothing is back here? You're crazy.*" Charlie tackled Roman to the ground again.

"*You don't have to be so aggressive.*" Roman nipped at his snout.

Charlie laid on top of him. "*You still smell good. I can't stop sniffing at you.*" Charlie stuck his nose against Roman's furry neck.

"*Charlie?*"

"*Yeah?*"

"*I don't want to be a wolf or a crow anymore. Please come with me to help the guys.*"

They rubbed noses, licking at each other's mouths. "*Okay, Roman. But you make sure no one kills us. Can you do that?*"

"*I'll try my best.*" Roman got to his feet and shook off, making his dark fur fluffy. "*By the way,*" Roman said as he began to trot in the direction of the search. "*I fuck you tonight. Doggie style.*"

"*Ha. Ha.*"

~

Roman didn't know if wolves could laugh, but he and Charlie were racing up the frozen trail, snapping at each other, tails flying high like flags, and making squeaking sounds as they did.

"You're enjoying this too much." He grabbed hold of Charlie's tail in his teeth and Charlie leapt up and sprinted off, showing his long canines to Roman as he did.

"And you're not?"

Roman caught up. *"Maybe a little. It is more fun with you."*

The helicopter flew low overhead. Both Roman and Charlie cowered and lay flat from the intensity of the noise. Roman crawled over to Charlie and pressed against his side for reassurance. *"Maybe this wasn't a good idea."*

"Too late now."

Charlie was staring up ahead.

A sheriff's deputy had a shotgun pointed at them.

"Shit. Where's Phil?" Roman didn't move.

"I can smell him but I can't see him."

Roman sniffed the air. *"He's by the fence with Nick."*

"He'll shoot if we run for it."

"He'll shoot if we don't. Ready?"

"Go!"

They took off and heard a shot ring out behind them. The noise was so loud to his sensitive ears, Roman nearly froze.

Charlie nipped at him to keep him moving. *"He's up there. He heard the shot and is coming to investigate it, Roman."*

"What's going on?" Phil yelled. "Who fired that gun?"

"Wolves! Look out!" The sheriff raised the gun to aim.

"Stop!" Phil held up his hand. "That's one of our agents!"

Roman put his front paws up on Phil's chest. *"Thanks, buddy."* He licked his face.

"Cut it out, Roman." Phil nudged him down. "Who's that?"

"Charlie." Roman danced around Charlie.

"Is he a real wolf?"

Roman made two squeaking noises, hoping Phil remembered their code from the other day.

"Then where did he come from?" Phil did.

"How do I tell him?" Roman stared at Charlie, who was sitting and panting, his tongue hanging out of his mouth.

"You're askin' me?" Charlie tilted his head sideways. *"I'm trying to prepare myself to be stark naked in front of a dozen people."*

Roman jumped up on Phil again. *"Let us help you. We have better noses than our tracking hounds."*

"I have no idea what you're trying to tell me." Phil shook his head in confusion.

"Charlie."

"Yeah?"

"Can you smell anything? Like burning herbs?" Roman stood beside him.

Charlie sniffed the air. *"I can. But I have no idea if it's just someone's fireplace to keep warm."*

"Not burning wood." Roman raised his nose in the air.

Phil knelt down. "Can you smell it?"

Roman made one noise. He could. He would never forget that smell. Trying to let Phil know, he made a circle at his feet.

"Go! We'll follow you."

Roman heard Phil using the radio to advise the officers on the scene Roman was going to track the scent.

Charlie caught up to Roman, who seemed to be making a beeline for the reservoir. *"You can smell the people who did this to you?"*

"I can smell the same chemical smell that knocked me out at the scene where this happened."

The noise of men running behind them, some on horseback, others on ATVs, clouded Roman's hearing, but not his sense of smell. Even as a human, he would never forget that odor.

He kept pace with Charlie, who was sniffing the air as he ran. *"You got it now?"*

"Yeah. I got it. Stinks to high heaven."

"I know." Roman cut through the thick trees that edged the water. He slowed down and could see a smoldering wisp of smoke.

Behind him a legion of men filled the area, signaling to one another to fan out. Roman could tell no humans were there.

A ring of stones, burnt offerings of herbs, what smelled like sulphur or something sour and heavy, and dead birds, tied at the feet with their throats cut. That was it.

Roman grew furious. *"No! This can't be!"*

"Roman...calm down."

He snarled and bit at the air in fury. Pain stabbed him. He fell to his side and began to writhe. The icy air reached his naked skin as he changed. In agony, he clawed at the ground and cried out. The canine whimpers caught in his throat and his deep voice grunting in pain replaced it.

As he made the transformation, Charlie stood over him, pressing his wet nose against his skin to comfort him.

Shivering, gasping for air, Roman opened his eyes to see Charlie's dark wolf eyes gazing at him, his ears perked upright.

Phil knelt beside them, giving Roman his jacket. "I'm sorry, Roman. But we must have missed them."

His emotions getting the better of him, Roman sat up, the jacket around his shoulders, and he sobbed. Charlie shifted on his paws, making whimpering sounds.

"Who is that, Roman?" Phil asked.

"It's Charlie."

The look on Phil's face was pure disbelief. "How?"

"How the hell should I know?" Roman petted Charlie's neck. "You gotta get mad, Charlie. That's the emotion these witches love the best."

Of Wolves and Men

Charlie snarled, snapping and making the hair raise on his back. Phil retreated but Roman stayed put. "That's my man."

Looking like a rabid wolf, Charlie began biting the low scrub, tearing it out by the roots with his teeth, shaking his head side to side.

"Get another coat, Phil. He's changing."

"Be right back."

Seeing the transformation from the outside was amazing. Roman crawled beside Charlie, trying to get him through the pain. "Hang on. You're almost there."

Charlie lay on his side, shivering from the cold. He spit the dirt out of his mouth and looked at Roman. "Am I insane or was I just a wolf?"

"Yes. You and me both." Roman rubbed his shoulder.

Phil returned with Nick's jacket and two yellow emergency blankets in plastic bags. Most of the men were photographing and taking evidence from the scene, but the few who had witnessed the wolf-to-man change were standing still with their mouths hanging open.

Butch rode up on Scout behind Phil and Nick. "Well, now you're two of a kind, Charlie. Looks like you won't be riding Spirit anymore."

Once he'd put the jacket on, Charlie wrapped the flimsy blanket around his waist. "Don't tell Vernon."

"Sure, Charlie. I'll leave you to do that." Butch tugged Scout's bridle and walked him away from the scene.

Roman touched Charlie's cheek. "Are you okay?"

"It was fun while it lasted."

"Don't worry. It'll be back. Just wait 'til you're a crow."

"Let me give you a ride to the cabin." Phil gestured to the two men.

Nick approached Roman. "We'll find them. The boys will submit the evidence for DNA and fingerprint testing. Someone is bound to be in the data base."

"Thanks, Nick. We'll get the jacket back to you."

"I'll stop by the cabin before I leave."

"Okay." Roman helped Charlie into one of the all terrain vehicles. The helicopter flew off, vanishing into the blue sky.

In silent contemplation, Roman was driven back to the trailhead where Phil's SUV was parked. When they arrived at the caravan of cars, Roman and Charlie sat in the back seat with the heat blasting, as Phil drove down the trail back to the ranch.

"What time is it?" Charlie asked.

"Eleven," Phil said.

"Maybe Vernon will get lucky and his tourists will miss the action."

"There's our clothing." Roman pointed.

Phil stopped the car and got out, gathering it.

"Charlie?" Roman squeezed his naked thigh. "Don't hate me."

"I don't hate you."

Phil opened the back seat and handed them their clothes.

"Thanks." Roman took the pile to sort through as Phil resumed their drive to the ranch house.

While they got dressed in the back seat, Roman tried to read Charlie's mind. But for some reason he couldn't any longer. The change had apparently made Charlie a closed book.

Chapter 15

Charlie had to admit visions of the 'simple life' began filling his head. Seeing the ranch house, Charlie knew Suzie and Sherlane were going to be around another week until they headed back to college. It made Charlie unhappy.

I'm sitting in an ATF agent's SUV, getting dressed after being naked on the cold ground, after being a wolf! Who needs this?

Charlie glanced at Roman as he put on his old, worn-out coat, one that was wearing through at the elbows. It should have been thrown out when he got his new one, but Charlie saved things like that.

Roman and Phil discussed the follow up to finding these 'witches' or whatever they were. Charlie didn't know if he cared.

If all it took to not change was to stay mellow, that made Charlie's life simple. He wasn't brought to anger easily. All through his early years he'd been calm and sensible. People came to him for help, advice, and ultimately he was made manager or boss wherever he worked.

When Phil parked in front of the ranch house, Charlie got out without a comment. He had work to do. There were tourists coming to ride in an hour.

"Charlie."

Hearing Roman's call, Charlie had half a mind to keep walking, but stopped and looked over his shoulder.

"Babe." Roman's tone softened as he approached, reaching out to hold Charlie's hands in his. "I'm sorry for dragging you into my mess."

"First of all, I'm not sure you are." Charlie tugged free of Roman's grip and said, "You used me to get help and now you don't need me anymore. So? Let me go on with my life. Okay?"

"That's not fair."

"Life ain't fair, Roman. You just learnin' that?" Charlie let out a sarcastic laugh and noticed Suzie and Sherlane staring at them through the front window of the living room. "I'll see ya later."

A hand held him back, squeezing his arm. Roman's warning filled in his ear, "Don't go with her."

Charlie wrenched his arm away and spun to face him. "You don't own me. You got that? Now go get in the damn car with your buddy and drive back to Reno."

"Stop taking this the wrong way. I'm crazy about you, but I want to get free of this curse. Can't you get that?"

"I get it! Okay? I'm the fucking curse you want to be free of. You think I'm stupid?"

"What are you talking about?"

The long line of black vehicles began leaving the ranch. Phil was idling the engine, as if waiting for Roman to return. Charlie didn't know what Roman's plans were and was afraid to ask. Vernon exited the ranch house to watch the exodus of officials.

"What did they do to the trail, Charlie?"

"The ground's so frozen, boss, it didn't mess it up much." Charlie asked, "What's the time?"

"Nearly noon. We have a group coming soon." Vernon addressed Roman, "When are you leaving?"

Without answering Vernon, Roman walked to the driver's side of the SUV to speak to Phil.

"I'm sorry, Vernon." Charlie stuffed his hands into his pockets. "I had no idea any of this would happen."

"I'm not sure I even know what's happening. Now Butch tells me you turned into a wolf too? What am I supposed to believe?"

Of Wolves and Men

Charlie rubbed his face in frustration. "I don't know. I thought I had my life together a few months back. Now I'm upside down." The SUV turned around in the lot and left the ranch. Roman watched it go. When it vanished, he walked the path in the direction of the cabins.

Suzie opened the door of the ranch house. "Come have a bite for lunch, Charlie." Harley raced out and sprinted up the trail, away from him. Charlie was amazed he didn't get attacked by the little terrier, but obviously Harley had other plans in mind.

Charlie was about to call Roman back to eat, but instead, he took off his hat and entered the house.

~

Roman shook off Charlie's jacket and tossed it on the couch. He sat with a mobile phone Phil had given him and dialed. "Mom?"

"Roman! My God! You're alive!"

He heard her shout to his father and her emotions brought a tear to Roman's eyes.

"Where are you? Hang on, Roman. Your dad's getting on the other line."

"Roman?"

"Hi, Dad." Roman slouched on Charlie's sofa, staring at the fireplace, knowing he should light a fire since the cold was infiltrating the wooden cabin.

"How are you? Where are you?"

"I'm okay. I'm hanging out on a ranch in Heber, Utah, for a bit."

"What happened to you? The agents at your office were very vague but they made it sound as if you were kidnapped."

"I sort of was, Dad." Roman had no idea how to explain his situation. "I'm okay now. They're just trying to find the suspects that did this to me."

"It's so good to hear your voice, Roman. I can't tell you how worried your father and sister were about you."

"I'm sorry, Mom. This is the first time I had a chance to call." He knelt next to the fireplace and tossed logs that were stacked beside it onto the grate. "Just don't worry anymore."

"Will you get any time off for Christmas?"

"No. I doubt it, Mom. But I'll call you when I can." He brushed his hand off on the sweatpants, staring at the spent ashes on the bottom of the hearth.

"I'm so glad you're all right."

He heard his mother crying. "I am. So don't worry anymore. Okay?"

"Do you still have your old phone number?" his dad asked.

"No. Let me give you this one since I know it came up blocked." He read the number engraved on it by the department and relayed the information to them. "I'll be in touch."

"Okay, son. You just take care and call as often as you can."

"I will, Dad. Love you guys." He hung up and set the phone behind him on the sofa, then lit kindling under the logs to get the fire burning. As it caught and crackled, he warmed his hands and sat with his back against the couch, staring at it.

He was attached to Charlie. Very much. If he had his way, Charlie would come back to Reno to live with him once he figured out how to get rid of the curse. *If* he had his way.

Unfortunately Charlie had a life too. And Charlie Mosby wasn't the kind of man to drop everything to be with him. Maybe that was a good thing. But as far as the future of their relationship went…it left few choices.

"Roman?"

Roman glanced at the door, hearing Suzie's voice.

"It's not locked."

She opened it and came in. "We prepared a nice lunch for everyone."

"I'm not feeling very welcome or sociable at the moment."

Looking concerned, Suzie crossed the room and stared into his eyes. "I've known Charlie for a few years. He's worth fighting for."

Roman smiled at the irony. "There's nothing I want more than to have Charlie live with me."

"Oh." She appeared confused.

"But I live and work in Reno, and he loves you guys and this job."

Suzie reached for Roman's arm and coaxed him to sit with her on the couch. "Butch said both of you turned into a wolf together. I didn't believe him."

"For once, Butch isn't lying. Charlie did too."

"No! How?"

"I don't know. But he did."

"Then you have to be together. Don't you see? It's fate trying to keep you as a pair."

"I'm not sure. I think it's bad luck by association. Charlie was unfortunate enough to be close to me, and now he's suffering for it."

"You must be hungry. Come join us."

"No. I'm sorry, Suzie. I just hate imposing on your good family. And Vernon is angry enough with the intrusion I created on his land this morning. I know you have a business to run."

After a moment where they just stared at each other, Suzie said, "Well, for what it's worth. I'm here if you need me."

"Thank you."

She stood and headed to the door. "And so is Charlie. If I were you? I'd never let that man go."

Roman smiled to himself. *If I were me, I wouldn't let him go either. But Charlie has a mind of his own.*

~

Charlie ate his pulled pork sandwich with JP, Goat, and Butch. Vernon and Sherlane were outdoors meeting and greeting the twelve o'clock trail riding group in the parking lot.

When Suzie entered the ranch house, she walked by the men and began filling a plastic plate with food.

Charlie knew what she was doing and guilt surfaced. "I'll take that to him, Suzie." He was caught off guard by the glare she shot at him. Knowing he wasn't winning brownie points with anyone here on the ranch any longer, Charlie didn't know what to do to get back to normal. Nothing felt normal anymore.

After she had filled the plate with everything Connie had cooked for their lunch, Suzie covered it with foil and stood still.

Charlie placed his empty plate in the sink. "Thank you, ma'am. It was delicious as usual."

"Anytime, Charlie."

He approached Suzie. "What'd I do now?" The plate was handed to him.

"Why don't you ask Roman that?" She turned her shoulder to him and began taking the empty plates from the table of men.

One by one the guys thanked the ladies for the meal, leaving to return to their work. Charlie caught Butch's eye before he put his hat on. The thoughts Charlie read from Butch were a mixture of jealousy and attraction. Charlie wasn't prepared for either.

As he headed outside, he tilted his hat against the brisk wind and avoided eye contact with the group of city folk that wanted a day of riding horses up in the hills. Charlie hoped they didn't run into any rude surprises, like an eviscerated deer.

The cabin door was slightly ajar when he touched the handle. A blazing fire in the hearth warmed the room making it feel inviting. Charlie heard the shower running and placed the plate of food on the kitchen table. He took off his hat and coat, craving a wash as well after frolicking in the hills on all fours.

Pressing his ear to the door, Charlie wondered why he felt like a stranger suddenly. He and Roman had made love a few times. But still he didn't know where he stood. And that was one of the most frustrating parts of loving Roman Burk.

Screw it.

Charlie opened the door and was hit with hot steam from the shower. Immediately, Roman poked his head out to look.

"I got food for you." Charlie thumbed his finger over his shoulder.

"Thanks."

The animal attraction between them was instant.

Roman dove at Charlie, grabbing him around the neck and bringing him to his lips. Charlie's clothing got drenched in water as he was drawn to Roman's wet body and the shower spray.

While Roman sucked at his mouth, Charlie began shedding his clothing, hopping to yank off his boots and socks.

Roman tore open his flannel shirt, spraying buttons across the small space.

His jeans and briefs yanked down and off his legs, Charlie stepped into the tub and encircled his arms around Roman's back, rocking him as they kissed. Roman shut the sliding door making their union private and cozy.

Maybe they had their problems to overcome, but Charlie knew he had never had sex like this in his life.

Keeping his balance as Roman began smoothing his hand down Charlie's chest to his abdomen, Charlie didn't want to stop kissing but had to catch his breath.

After taking a deep inhale of air, he watched Roman. Charlie spread his legs and held onto the wall for support. Roman kissed his way down Charlie's tight six-pack to his treasure trail, lapping the base of his cock.

An instant surge of pleasure brought the slight ache of his body wanting to change. The wolf in him was beating at the door to get out. Though Charlie would have liked to be the powerful *canis lupus* again, he wouldn't trade the man on man sex between him and Roman for anything.

Roman's jet black hair was dripping wet as he closed his eyes and opened his mouth. Charlie's cock engorged quickly at the sight. Using one hand Roman held the base of Charlie's dick, the other he toyed with Charlie's balls, rolling the wet sack in his fingers. Between the visual stimulation and the physical, Charlie was on the edge. "I'm almost there."

Roman moaned, echoing in the wet room and sucked faster, harder, jacking Charlie's cock to get him to come.

And he did. Charlie arched his back to deepen his penetration into Roman's mouth, closing his eyes and holding tight to Roman's shoulders. The climax was so powerful, Charlie's legs gave out.

Roman let out a low snarl and stood, flipping Charlie to face the wall with the shower head. Charlie pressed his palms on the wet tile and gasped as Roman penetrated him. He looked down at Roman's arms as they held him around the waist. The slippery soap was keeping him lubricated, but Charlie didn't know for how long. Again he cursed himself for not being diligent and buying rubbers and lube, but life had become so crazy, he couldn't manage to get away from the ranch for long…and would never ask anyone to pick those things up for him.

The snarls became deeper and the fucking, rougher. Charlie grew slightly angry at Roman for not breaking him in gently the first time they had made love. Charlie still wasn't used to this kind of violent sex and felt as if he were nearly a virgin to man on man loving. Charlie would have preferred being introduced slowly and screwed gently from now on. But asking a wolf to fuck slower was absurd.

"Easy, Roman." Charlie tried to ride it out. When the opposite happened, and Roman increased the depth and speed of his thrusting, Charlie's top lip curled and he snarled.

Just as he was pinned to the wall and Roman's cock gave up its load inside him, Charlie spun around violently and the two of them smashed around inside the wet stall as wolves.

Roman leapt up, banging against the glass slider and shimmying out of the gap opening of the door.

Of Wolves and Men

Charlie nipped at his heels in fury as Roman raced around the cabin trying to avoid him.

"Get back here!"

"No!"

"Roman! Say you're sorry!"

"For what?"

Roman spun around when he was cornered, his hair standing on end and his teeth showing.

Charlie confronted him, his tail straight up in a show of dominance. *"For fucking me too hard."* He bared his fangs.

"You think I can help it? I can't believe we're not using condoms and lube." Roman shook off the water and sat on his haunches. *"I'm sorry, Charlie. I am."*

Charlie gave his fur a shake to get the water off as well, then lay in front of the fire to warm. *"There's food for you on the table."*

Roman walked to the kitchen, put his paws on the chair and began chewing off the foil wrapper.

Blinking his eyes, Charlie stared at the flames and sighed. Maybe being a wolf wasn't so much fun after all. He glanced over his shoulder to see Roman eating off the plate, licking it clean.

Roman joined him, lying in front of the fire to dry their fur and keep warm. Charlie licked at his mouth affectionately.

"That food is good. I can see why you want to stay here." Roman raised his snout as Charlie lapped at him.

"I suppose I just don't have any reason to leave." Charlie rolled against Roman and put his paws out in front of him to look at them. *"Man, I have big feet."*

"Do...do you want a reason to leave the ranch?"

Charlie connected with Roman's green eyes. *"I don't know what I want."* Charlie began growing upset and angry at their dilemma. He instantly began to feel pain from the emotion.

As Charlie curled up in a ball and whimpered, Roman reacted to his pain and did the same.

The change came and they suffered through it and ended up lying naked together on the hearth rug, gasping for air and moaning.

"Wow, that never gets easy." Charlie rubbed his head and arms, shaking off the echoes of the pain. "So? When am I going to be a crow and get to fly?"

"Hell if I know." Roman propped up his head in his hand and caressed Charlie's damp hair. "Charlie."

"Yeah?"

"You do mean a lot to me."

"What do you want me to do?" Charlie resumed his position, lying against Roman's side.

"I can't ask you to make sacrifices for me. All I do want to from you, is that you put everything on hold until we figure out how to get out of this curse. Is that too much to ask?"

Charlie sighed deeply. *Was it?* "No. It's not too much to ask."

"Thank you, Charlie." Roman reached for a kiss.

He met Roman's lips and then relaxed once more against him. *Just get through this curse. Then...Then what?*

Charlie didn't know how long it would take the agents to find the suspects. He didn't know if this change was permanent, and if it was, he certainly couldn't expect Spirit to allow him on his back. So that meant he couldn't do his job. And if he couldn't do his job, he was useless to Vernon.

Even though Roman couldn't read his mind, he obviously could see Charlie brooding. "Stop analyzing it. You'll go nuts."

Charlie took a deep breath. "I can't help it. A week ago I thought the craziest thing I ever did was get my cock sucked by a gay boy on Interstate 80. Now?"

"I would have liked to have been the voyeur in that deed."

"Yeah. You would have." Charlie repositioned so he was facing Roman, mirroring his posture of lying on his side with his head propped up on his palm. The firelight gave Roman's skin a silky glow, and his eyes gleamed. "I suppose whatever happens, happens."

"It's how I'm trying to play it." Roman caressed Charlie's arm.

Charlie scooted closer, connecting their lower halves together as he kissed Roman. The heat from Roman's crotch lit another fire in Charlie. "I can't deny I'm happy we met. Even with all the challenges."

"Challenges? I suppose that's the polite way to put it."

"We don't know what tomorrow will bring."

"I do. A wolf or a crow. I know it will be one of those."

Charlie smiled though thinking about the future at the moment was scaring him a little. "Hold me. Can you do that?"

"I can do that." Roman took Charlie into his arms.

Charlie closed his eyes and rested his head on Roman's. He felt his breathing, inhaled his scent, and knew no matter what form they took, whether it be wolves or men, he would love Roman. Forever.

The End

G. A. Hauser

Stay tuned for the sequel;

THE ORDER OF WOLVES

Blurb and Sample Chapter of The Order of Wolves:

In the sequel to *Of Wolves and Men* we find ATF Agent Roman Burk and horse wrangler Charlie Mosby, still investigating the strange curse they have been burdened with.

Charlie struggles to come to terms with his boss and co-workers on the horse ranch in Heber, Utah, knowing he is Roman's gay lover. This new problem of changing into a wolf or crow whenever they grow angry or emotional, has both Charlie and Roman near the end of their rope.

Roman loves Charlie, but he loves his job back in Reno as well. Though Charlie has been his champion and ally through their ordeal, Roman doesn't know if Charlie would be willing to give up his life and career and join him in the city.

Another wrangler, Butch Crowell complicates the situation for the two men, whose life is already too bizarre for either of them to believe. Butch instills jealousy in Roman as he too becomes enamored with the handsome cowboy Charlie.

In the end, it's up to Charlie to decide which path to choose, and if leaving a place where he has lived and worked for years is the best course of action.

The Order of Wolves is about the alpha male, and who will inevitably be top dog.

Sample Chapter for The Order of Wolves:

Of Wolves and Men

Look at you. Charlie hadn't always preferred men as sexual partners. He had dated women exclusively, and at one time considered the idea of asking out one of Vernon's lovely daughters, Suzie or Sherlane. But...

A chance meeting on the roadside on Interstate 80 with a gay man changed all that. 'Joe' offered Charlie a blowjob after helping him change a flat tire. Charlie couldn't recall the last time anyone had offered him such a lovely treat, so he accepted, assuming doing something once with a man was curiosity, nothing more. But after the contact, Charlie was left craving another sexual encounter with a man.

That's when he met Roman, who he found stark naked on ranch property. The sexual appetite of Roman, not to mention his good looks, gave Charlie another chance to see if... If an alternative lifestyle was something he could consider.

It was.

The closer he and Roman got, the less Charlie craved lying with a woman.

And now? Now that they were both half wolf/ half man, or a third wolf, a third crow, (which Charlie had yet to change into) and a third man. *What on earth are we?*

Charlie's sexual drive had hit an all time peak. All he wanted to do was hump Roman, suck him, roll on him, and sniff him. It was madness at its highest level, and pure fantasy.

With his morning erection needing some attention, Charlie dug one hand under Roman and curled him into an embrace. Slowly Roman came to the surface of his slumber. His bedroom brown eyes opened under dark lashes, making Charlie shiver with desire.

"Howdy, partner." Charlie smiled, giving Roman's neck a good sniff.

"That's some wake-up call." Roman parted his legs and pressed their crotches together.

"Rise n' shine." Charlie licked Roman's jaw, beginning to assert his dominance over him, urging Roman to his back.

A sound like a low purr came from Roman as he submitted to Charlie's advance. Spreading wide, he allowed Charlie to do as he pleased, which made Charlie a happy man.

Once Charlie had licked his way down to Roman's chest, giving attention to each nipple, he knelt up and reached for the petroleum jelly left on his nightstand. Though he had intentions of getting condoms and proper lubrication, Charlie wasn't one to go into town very often, and the idea of asking someone to pick those items up for him was impossible. Not to mention, turning into something canine while behind the wheel of his truck, was a daunting prospect. It was against Charlie's nature to take risks, but he was a very trusting man. He trusted Roman.

As Roman watched Charlie prepare, he said, "We have got to get lube. I can't stand that shit."

Charlie chuckled softly. "Read my mind?"

"No. I can't seem to do that to you anymore. But, come on." He curled his nose.

"Lubrication and condoms. I must be outa my mind to be ridin' you bareback."

"Me? I'm clean. Are you kidding me?" Roman shifted on the bed as Charlie inserted two fingers inside him. "Oh, that's nice…" He moaned. "And I haven't had sex for years before we met. Not with this crazy job, I don't."

"Hush up. I'm not believin' that for a minute." Charlie tried to wipe his fingers off and ended up rubbing the remainder into his dry hands. He tugged on his cock to keep it hard, moving closer.

"Right. You believe we turn into animals but you don't believe I don't fuck around anymore. I give up."

"Fuck now, talk later." Charlie rocked Roman's legs backwards so he exposed his ass, pointing his stiff length at it.

Roman held his own knees and raised his hips to make it easier for Charlie. Instead, Charlie backed up, grabbed Roman and spun him around roughly. "Changed my mind. I'm goin' to do you doggie style."

"How appropriate." Roman got on his hands and knees.

"Seems more natural."

"Don't even go there." Roman pushed his face into the pillow.

"I'm goin' there, Roman. Make no mistake." Charlie laughed and gripped Roman around his hips, yanking him closer. He pushed the head of his cock against Roman's tight rim and penetrated him gently.

Roman gave a snarl and wriggled backwards, uniting their bodies.

G. A. Hauser

About the Author

Award-winning author G.A. Hauser was born in Fair Lawn, New Jersey, USA and attended university in New York City. She moved to Seattle, Washington where she worked as a patrol officer with the Seattle Police Department. In early 2000 G.A. moved to Hertfordshire, England where she began her writing in earnest and published her first book, In the Shadow of Alexander. Now a full-time writer, G.A. has written over fifty novels, including several best-sellers of gay fiction and is an Honorary Board Member of Gay American Heroes for her support of the foundation. For more information on other books by G.A., visit the author at her official website. www.authorgahauser.com

G.A. has won awards from All Romance eBooks for Best Author 2009, Best Novel 2008, *Mile High*, and Best Author 2008, Best Novel 2007, *Secrets and Misdemeanors*, Best Author 2007.

Of Wolves and Men

The G.A. Hauser Collection

Single Titles

Unnecessary Roughness

Hot Rod

Of Wolves and Men

The Order of Wolves

Mr. Right

My Best Friend's Boyfriend

The Diamond Stud

The Hard Way

Games Men Play

Born to Please

Got Men?

Heart of Steele

All Man

Julian

Black Leather Phoenix

London, Bloody, London

In The Dark and What Should Never Be, Erotic Short Stories

Mark and Sharon (formally titled A Question of Sex)

A Man's Best Friend

It Takes a Man

G. A. Hauser

The Physician and the Actor
For Love and Money
The Kiss
Naked Dragon
Secrets and Misdemeanors
Capital Games
Giving Up the Ghost
To Have and To Hostage
Love you, Loveday
The Boy Next Door
When Adam Met Jack
Exposure
The Vampire and the Man-eater
Murphy's Hero
Mark Antonious deMontford
Prince of Servitude
Calling Dr Love
The Rape of St. Peter
The Wedding Planner
Going Deep
Double Trouble
Pirates

Of Wolves and Men

Miller's Tale

Vampire Nights

Teacher's Pet

In the Shadow of Alexander

The Rise and Fall of the Sacred Band of Thebes

The Action Series

Acting Naughty

Playing Dirty

Getting it in the End

Behaving Badly

Dripping Hot

Packing Heat

Being Screwed

Something Sexy

Going Wild

Men in Motion Series

Mile High

Cruising

Driving Hard

Leather Boys

G. A. Hauser

Heroes Series

Man to Man
Two In Two Out
Top Men

G.A. Hauser
Writing as Amanda Winters

Sister Moonshine

Nothing Like Romance

Silent Reign

Butterfly Suicide

Mutley's Crew

A quickie based on the characters of ***The Boy Next Door.***

<u>Summer Love</u>

"You know the cops come by every night here to check on the pool."

"Why are you so paranoid, Brandon? This isn't the first time we've skinny dipped." Zach tread water in the deep end of Memorial Pool.

Brandon reached onto 'the raft', a plateau in the middle of the man-made lake. "Yeah, but there's a big difference from skinny-dipping in your backyard and here in the damn town pool. We can't get arrested in your backyard."

"Brandy, the night is hot and muggy, no one is around, and we're completely hidden behind this thing." Zachary reached out to hold the wooden frame of the raft. "Why don't you just relax and kiss me?"

Chuckling nervously, Brandon could see Zach's blue eyes in the dim light of the reflections on the pool. "It's over ten feet deep here, Zach. If we kiss I may sink."

"I've got you." Zach wrapped his legs around Brandon's under the water.

"You know, you're trouble. Before we got into this insanity I was a good son. Now? I'm stripping off my clothing at night in the town pool."

"All the seniors do it. It's tradition."

"Get over here, Zachary Sherman."

When Zach's mouth met his, Brandon was sure the heat they were producing would cause the water to boil around them. They were mad. They were impulsive, but it was summer, and they were in love.

Of Wolves and Men

Moments after the kiss, Zach climbed onto the raft boldly standing naked in the dim spotlights. "I'm king of the world!" Zach shouted, beating his chest.

Loving every minute of it, Brandon met him on that dry wooden float, wrapping around his body around Zach's. "You are insane."

After kissing Brandon, Zachary broke the embrace and sprinted off the dock, diving into the deep water. Racing after him, Brandon swam as fast as he could catch him, his heart hopelessly lost, and completely in love.

G. A. Hauser

RECOMMENDED READ FROM STORMY GLENN;
SYNOPSIS; Love Sexy True Blood Mate 3
AVAILABLE: Tuesday, March 29th
[Siren Classic ManLove: Erotic Alternative Paranormal Romance, M/M, shape-shifters, werewolves]

Logan Stone lives a lonely existence as the beta of his wolf clan. It's his job to protect his people and follow out the orders of his alpha. That doesn't leave much time to find a mate or fill the empty hole in his heart. When he spots a set of sexy eyes staring at him during the moon festival, Logan knows he has met his mate.

Finding Love Star is not as easy as keeping him. Love may be fascinated by all things wolf but when Logan goes feral during their mating, Love runs for his life. Logan has to call for help to find Love, only discover his mate is hiding right under his nose at the Stone Clan compound.

Instead of convincing Love of the merits of being mated to a wolf, Logan has to depend on Love to protect himself even as he tries to shield the man from the dangerous world he has just entered. If they survive the interference of well meaning friends and a coyote shifter bent on killing Love, they just might have a chance of finding out what fate has planned for them.

SAMPLE CHAPTER;

He couldn't wait to get rid of his jeans and feel those hands against his bare skin. Hell, he couldn't wait to feel all of Logan against his bare skin. As big as Logan was, Love had no doubt that he could cover his smaller body from head to toe, and then some.

Love yelped in surprise as he was suddenly lowered to the ground. He barely had time to steady himself on his feet before hands were pulling at his clothes. Within moments, Love found himself standing before Logan naked as the day he was born.

The low rough rumble emanating from Logan told Love that the man liked what he saw. It vibrated through Love's body, energizing him, arousing him. He looked up into Logan's eyes, and his breath caught in his throat.

Logan's amber eyes had gone deep golden brown. His lip curled back, showing off his perfect white teeth. But it was the savage snarl on Logan's face as he gazed down at his naked body that really set Love off.

Love held his arms out to his sides. "If you plan on just staring at me, this relationship is going to take more work than I thought."

The moment the words were out of Love's mouth he wished he could take them back. Logan's eyes flashed to his as a slow, wicked grin crossed his lips. Some intuitive gut feeling told Love that he had just become the prey to a hunter.

Going purely on instinct, Love turned and ran. He didn't get two steps before two large arms encircled him from behind and pulled him back against Logan's hard body. Love's felt a shudder shoot through his body as long teeth scraped across the back of his neck.

"Logan," Love groaned. "That is so fucking hot!"

His hands moved back behind his head to wrap around Logan's neck. He tilted his head to one side, giving Logan unobstructed access to the side of his throat. It was a submissive gesture. Love knew that, but he was helpless to stop it. Something in him demanded that he submit. Love could no more deny that powerful demand than he could have stopped breathing.

Of Wolves and Men

Long fingers encircled Love's hard cock, stroking him furiously just as sharp teeth bit into the soft flesh between his neck and shoulder. Shock rocked through him as he realized Logan bit him, but he still cried out as the combination of pleasure and pain overwhelmed him.

A thick thigh moved between Love's legs and pressed tightly against him from behind. Small keening sounds escaped from his lips. Every touch of Logan's hands and body against his was like a burning flame. Love wanted to be consumed. He wanted to burn for Logan.

His hands clenched in Logan's sunlight blond hair, pulling at the long locks in desperation. He could feel Logan sucking on his neck, marking him, claiming him, but he needed more. He needed…he needed…

"Logan!" Love begged. "Fuck me!"

The teeth in his neck withdrew. Love was pushed down onto the ground, landing on his hands and knees. Before he could protest the rough treatment, Logan's fingers pushed into his tight hole.

"Aaahhh, fuck yes!" Love cried out.

Logan began stretching him, adding another finger, then another. Some part of Love wondered where the man got lube, but he was too overcome with burning sensation to really care.

He was just thankful because he felt pretty sure Logan was about to fuck him into the ground.

Love felt Logan pull his fingers away and press his massive cock into him. He could hear Logan's heavy breathing as he thrust into Love's tight grasp. The rough material of Logan's jeans brushed against the back of his thighs. He could smell Logan's arousal permeating the air around them.

Love groaned, his head dropping forward. He could feel the small bar piercing just under the head of Logan's cock when the man thrust into him. It seemed to know right where Love's sweet spot was located and pegged it every time.

Having sex wasn't something new to Love, but despite what Mick had said, he didn't fuck anything that walked. Still, there was something distinctively different about being fucked by Logan. He felt like he was being claimed and not just fucked, like somehow Logan was placing a stamp of ownership on him.

Everything felt different, more intense. As Logan pounded into him, Love felt every movement of Logan's body, every single breath that came out of Logan's mouth. Love could feel his orgasm building deep within his body and knew that it was going to be spectacular. Logan was going to consume him.

Of Wolves and Men

When Logan's teeth bit into his shoulder again, Love knew it was over for him. His fingers curled into the cold dirt beneath him as streaks of pleasure exploded throughout his entire body.

BIO FOR STORMY GLENN;

I'm a writer of erotic, paranormal, werewolf, vampire, futuristic, fantasy, suspense, contemporary, gay, and Ménage a Trois romances. I'm currently published with Siren Publishing, Torquere Press, Noble Romance Publishing, and Silver Publishing. I create stories, romances, and dreams because that's what I believe in. I also believe the only thing sexier than a man in cowboy boots is two, or three men in cowboy boots. I believe in love at first sight, soul mates, true love, and happy endings and that's what I like to write about.

http://www.bookstrand.com/love-sexy

CPSIA information can be obtained at www.ICGtesting.com
Printed in the USA
LVOW011321120911

245931LV00005B/12/P

9 781461 020141